"I don't see how we can pretend she's invisible."

That's what one of the girls said about Trina, whom nobody liked.

But pretend they did, teasing her and giggling. Sandy, the newcomer, found herself hanging back from the other tormentors. She knew the game Melissa was playing with Trina was mean, and she didn't want to take part in it.

But Melissa, the popular blond leader whom all the girls followed, was insistent. She waved to Sandy.

"It's your turn. Go ahead."

"I don't want to," Sandy said.

Melissa's smile never lost its sweetness. *You'd better, you know. Otherwise you might become invisible too . . . !"*

Nobody Likes Trina

by
Phyllis A. Whitney

Ⓢ
A SIGNET BOOK
NEW AMERICAN LIBRARY
TIMES MIRROR

SIGNET TRADEMARK REG. U.S. PAT. OFF. AND FOREIGN COUNTRIES
REGISTERED TRADEMARK—MARCA REGISTRADA
HECHO EN CHICAGO, U.S.A.

SIGNET, SIGNET CLASSICS, MENTOR, PLUME, MERIDIAN AND NAL
BOOKS are published by The New American Library, Inc.,
1633 Broadway, New York, New York 10019

FIRST SIGNET PRINTING, APRIL, 1976

7   8   9   10   11   12   13   14   15

PRINTED IN THE UNITED STATES OF AMERICA

With many thanks to my advisers—
teacher supervisors Marion Ramsbotham and
Evangeline Nolder, teacher Ralph Christiano,
and librarian Dot Henry

And with special thanks to my granddaughter
Barbara Jahnke, who gave me the idea
for the story

Contents

1

Moving Day

Moving day was nearly over. All around the new house furniture stood in strange places and boxes were piled upon boxes. The vans and the burly moving men were gone, the men having been handsomely tipped by Ted Forster, Sandy's father. In the living room Sandy's mother, Jenny, sat on a packing case and stared out the big picture windows at a bleak December day. It was late afternoon on a Friday, and the light was beginning to fade.

In another room Dad was exuberantly setting up one of the beds that would be put to use that night, banging around and whistling cheerfully. Nothing could make him happier than to leave the dirt and grime and heavy air of New York City, and move out here to the clean New Jersey countryside. He had grown increasingly more cheerful with every mile they left behind, while Mother had become more and more apprehensive. Now as her mother sat on the packing case and stared out at the fog-obscured view, Sandy was aware of her discouragement, sensing that she was close to tears.

Sandy had dark eyes that were very like her mother's, and they had the same stricken look about them now. Her long black hair, worn loose under a green velvet band, had grown tangled during the day, somehow adding to her look of discouragement. Ordinarily she was a cheerful girl with a quick smile and wide-awake eyes. But now she felt uncertain, concerned, even a little frightened, and it was hard to endure Dad's rather noisy good cheer.

She went to stand beside her mother, and Jenny Forster gave her a quick, understanding look and forced a smile.

"It's too bad the fog has closed us in. I want you to see the view. You'd never guess that straight out there, ten miles away, is the Delaware Water Gap. The hill in front of the house slants so steeply that you can see over ridges and valleys in between, right to the mountains that make the Gap."

Sandy didn't care about the view at the moment. There were no nearby houses in sight—only thick woods that crowded all around. Familiar city sounds had been left behind long ago. Here there was such a quiet outdoors that it almost pressed upon her ears, like cotton stuffed into them.

Mother saw her expression and moved over on the packing case so Sandy could sit beside her. "It's going to be an adventure, you know—learning a whole new way of life. Making new friends, finding wonderful new things to do."

Sandy looked thoughtfully into her mother's face. "You were nearly crying," she accused.

Mother blinked long lashes rapidly and sprang up from the packing case, stretching her legs in their denim pants, stretching her arms over her head.

"I'm just tired. Moving's always an ordeal. We'll all feel better tomorrow."

Sandy thought of her lost friends, whom she might never see again. She thought of bright, busy streets, where something was always going on, of the city where there were parks and museums and theaters and the small private school to which she had gone. She and Mother had both lived in cities all their lives. Dad had been born on an Iowa farm and had grown up in the country. This was like a homecoming for him. He had begun to hate his job with an advertising company, begun to hate having to write ecstatic copy about detergents and motor oil and the latest electric gadgets. He didn't need to feel any better tomorrow—he was already right up there at the top, bursting with delight over this change. Somehow, to Sandy it didn't seem quite fair. Jenny Forster's friends had been left behind too, and so many things she had loved doing in the city. It seemed to Sandy that it was two Forsters against one. Two who loved the city and just one who wanted to live in the country—yet it was the one who had won out.

Mother moved about the room, gesturing rather more than was necessary, as though she tried to build up her own courage. "Don't you think the long sofa will be fine against that back wall, Sandy? When we sit there we can look straight out at the view, and the fireplace will be close on our left. We'll hang our big picture of autumn woods in New England over the sofa, and the snow scene above the mantel. In no time at all it will begin to feel like home."

Sandy stayed where she was on the packing case and

hunched herself over, pulling her knees up to her chin and closing her eyes tightly, so that not a tear could squeeze itself out.

"Honey," Mother said from across the room, "we *will* make new friends, you know. It's just right now when we're tired, and everything is in a mess, and we haven't met anyone yet, that it seems hard. It's going to be a lovely new life. You'll see."

"You didn't want to come," Sandy said, letting her long black hair fall over her face to hide it.

Mother crossed the room, her loafers making sharp little clicks on the bare floor. "Of course I wanted to come. I couldn't bear the way Dad was working day after day in an office he hated, just to take care of us. A family is a partnership—it has to work out what is best for everyone. When this opportunity for your father to buy into a small-town hardware store came up, we had to help him take it."

"Hardware!" Sandy said. "What's so wonderful about hardware?"

"Just that he likes to make things, build things. He can learn the hardware business easily because he already knows a lot about it. But out here it won't have to be his whole life, the way an advertising company on Madison Avenue has to be. Here we've got the outdoors around us—and that's where he loves to be. He's spent years giving *us* the city. Now it's our turn to give him the country."

With the reasonable part of her mind, Sandy accepted this, went along with it. Everything had been talked over thoroughly before they made this move. It had even seemed rather exciting at first. But that was before the actual parting from everything she had known and understood—where even the dangers were those she was familiar with. Here there was no one close by. Not a nearby house could be seen out there in the gathering dusk. The loneliness was a little frightening.

Dad's cheerful whistling came closer, burst into the room and was cut off as he saw them sitting there in the dim light, while the December afternoon faded and the fog pressed closely at the windows.

"Hey!" he said. "What's everybody sitting here in the dark for? Can't we set up a lamp or two? Better still, I'll light the fire. Mr. Seale left us a good stock of birch logs when he moved out."

Sandy watched her father as he stepped buoyantly

around the room. He was tall and broad-shouldered—he'd played football back at the State University of Iowa. He had a shock of brown hair that fell over one eye, and a tooth with a chipped corner that somehow made his smile endearing. She watched him with a strange mingling of love and resentment as he busied himself at the fireplace with paper and kindling, opening the draft to the chimney, striking a match. In no time flames leaped in the stone fireplace, and the crackling of the wood made a cheerful sound.

"How about that?" Dad said. "Our first fire in our new home!"

Sandy and her mother turned toward the blaze, but they found it hard to match his exuberance. He came over to kiss Jenny on the cheek and rumple Sandy's hair.

"How'll it be if I play cook tonight and open some delicious cans of spaghetti and meatballs? My chef's special! Nourishment is a sure cure for long faces."

Mother smiled. "You're writing ad copy again, Ted! Anyway, I'll take you up on that. Let's go out to the kitchen and see if we can locate the barrel with the pots and pans. Will you help, Sandy?"

Sandy remained on the packing case. Somehow she didn't feel cooperative, and she wasn't one bit hungry.

Dad spoke to her gently. "I can't wait to show you what the country's like. And by tomorrow I think you'll have made at least two or three friends. I understand there's a girl about your age living down the road a little way in one direction—Trina Carpozi. And the other way, between us and the highway, the Wendels live, and they have an older boy, Cliff. I met him when I came out here the first time, and he seems a good kid. Mr. Wendel will probably be your homeroom teacher in school. Then, of course, there'll be Melissa Morris. Mrs. Morris' house is out on the highway, a little farther from Halcyon than we are. Her daughter, Melissa, is in your class, too."

Mrs. Morris was the widow into whose hardware store in the village of Halcyon, Dad was buying. But nobody lived really close, as Sandy's best friend had in the same apartment building in New York. She followed her parents to the kitchen and looked around.

Their new house was modern—a long ranch style, with everything on one floor, except the basement laundry and furnace room. The kitchen seemed less in a muddle than the rest of the rooms because so much was built-in. The refrigerator and eye-level oven were turquoise blue, and the handsome cabinets above the sink and counters were of dark birch, smooth and polished. The moving men had dumped Mother's round wooden dinette table and chairs in the big kitchen and Sandy helped to shove them over beside windows that looked out on what might be a view when the fog went away. The former owners had left all their curtains and draperies up throughout the house, so the kitchen, with its turquoise-and-brown-printed curtains had a trim look in spite of packing boxes and the barrel in which Mother was rummaging.

Sandy had not seen the house until today, since it hadn't been convenient for her to come out with them when they were purchasing. Her parents had tried their best to describe everything and make her feel that she knew the place ahead of time, but nothing had really worked. To Sandy it all seemed strange and not very friendly. Mr. and Mrs. Seale had built the house and lived on their hundred acres of mountainside for the last few years. His work as a naturalist had taken him to another part of the country recently, and they had been forced to sell the home they loved. But it wasn't the Forster home. Not yet.

"Everything I want is at the bottom!" Mother wailed, leaning over the barrel's rim while she tossed out wads of newspaper packing.

The chime of the doorbell startled them and for a moment the three Forsters stared at one another. Then Dad went to turn on an outside light and open the front door. Sandy looked into the hallway that separated living room, dining room, and kitchen from the rear bedrooms. She saw a woman and a slim blond girl coming into the house at Dad's invitation.

Mother tucked a flyaway strand of black hair into the French twist at the back of her head, and came to look over Sandy's shoulder. "That's Mrs. Morris and Melissa," she whispered, and went forward to welcome the visitors.

Mrs. Morris was short and rather plump, and she wore checked slacks and a brown sweater. She carried a large paper bag, which she bore into the kitchen and set down on a counter. Her graying hair had been blown untidy on the way in from the car, and her face, as Sandy was to learn, wore a perpetually worried look.

"Thought you might enjoy a ready-cooked meal tonight," she told them. "I just took this casserole out of the oven, and it's still bubbly hot. Meat and macaroni. Put it in your oven to keep warm till you're ready for dinner."

"You couldn't be more welcome!" Mother said. "This is awfully kind of you. Hello, Melissa. I'd like you to meet my daughter, Sandra."

After a first quick glance at Mrs. Morris, Sandy had not taken her eyes from the blond girl who followed her mother into the kitchen. She was very pretty, with her fair hair a cap of soft natural curls about her head—nothing the wind would tangle the way it did straight hair. She wore blue jeans and a pale-blue sweater, and somehow she looked older than Sandy had expected. She behaved with a sureness that set her apart, and made Sandy feel suddenly awkward and shy. After all, she was moving into this girl's territory, and she wasn't sure of anything—whereas Melissa Morris was obviously sure of just who she was and where she stood.

At Jenny Forster's introduction, Melissa turned casually to look at Sandy—as if she had not noticed her before, and she smiled sweetly, though to Sandy the smile didn't seem very real.

"Hello, Sandra," she said, and looked away at once.

"Everybody calls me Sandy." It seemed best to make an effort to be friendly, though Melissa gave her an odd feeling of uncertainty.

The other girl did not seem to hear. She had already turned her attention upon her elders, as though she found Sandy of no consequence, and was more interested in watching Mrs. Forster light the turquoise oven and set the casserole in it.

"Do you think you'll like living in the country?" Mrs. Morris asked Mother. She seemed more ill at ease than her daughter—perhaps because of her daughter.

"Of course we'll like it," Mother said readily. "Though we may need a little time to get used to it. Ted knows all about country living, but we don't, do we, Sandy?"

Thus drawn in, Sandy nodded without speaking. She was still thinking about Melissa, watching her, wondering how you got to be friends when you were the stranger coming into a new place.

"You'll be starting school on Monday, I expect?" Mrs. Morris said.

Again Sandy nodded. It seemed especially difficult to be starting school in the middle of the term.

"Probably you'll be in Mr. Wendel's room," Mrs. Morris went on, speaking quickly as if she wanted to cover up Melissa's indifference.

Sandy began to feel a little indignant and she tried to find a way to assert herself with Melissa, to show her she was not dependent upon her for friendship.

"There's another girl living on this road, isn't there?" she asked. "A girl named Trina Carpozi?"

"Yes—" Mrs. Morris sounded doubtful. "Yes, there is. She lives just out of sight in that old Moravian stone house that was built a couple of hundred years ago. But I don't know if—that is—her mother's dead. And nobody knows what happened to her father. She lives with her grandparents, and I'm not sure—"

"Being this close will be fine for both Trina and Sandy, I'm sure." Mother had broken into Mrs. Morris' strange floundering. "I'm glad there's another girl close to her own age nearby."

Melissa made an odd, snorting sound, and Sandy looked at her quickly. It was hard to tell whether she had suppressed a laugh, or made a sound of mocking.

"Now then, Lissa, honey," her mother said. "Just because you and Trina don't get along—"

"As if anybody could get along with *her!*" said Melissa.

Mrs. Morris hurried to speak of other things, and in a few moments she and her daughter took their leave. Dad told her he'd see her tomorrow at the store and that he looked forward to getting involved in the business.

"I'll take a chain saw to a typewriter any day," he assured Mrs. Morris cheerfully, as he saw her and Melissa to the door.

"How did you like Melissa?" Dad asked Sandy when the Morrises had gone.

Sandy felt a little grumpy. "How do I know? She didn't seem much interested in meeting me."

"She's probably shy," Mother said. "After all, you're the girl from New York, and she's lived in the country all her life. She may feel a little uncertain about you at first."

Sandy said nothing. She couldn't explain her feeling that Melissa wasn't uncertain about anything, and that she was holding back from being friendly with some deliberate intent. She felt sorry and disappointed. Mother had talked a lot about her being friends with Melissa Morris, and now it didn't look as though this would be possible.

"Do you need me for anything now?" she asked her mother.

Jenny Forster was unwrapping plates and cups and table silver, and Sandy knew very well that she ought to help. She had an almost overpowering need to get off by herself and think about things, however. Sometimes you just had to stop and take a deep breath and get used to what was happening.

"Your mother can use an extra pair of hands—" Dad began, but Mother shook her head.

"Run along, Sandy. I'll put you to work on the dishes after dinner."

"Do you mean I can go outside?"

"If you want to. And if you don't stay too long. Better not wander far from the house until you know the grounds better. And you may need to put on a jacket. It can get cold here on the mountain at night."

Sandy went out of the room quickly before any further warnings or suggestions could be made. The front door was at one end of the long house and opened onto a small porch with three steps leading down to a walk. It wasn't very cold outside, and her sweater was enough. She followed the walk out to the driveway, where the garage stood, a wide parking space of paved blacktop opening in front of it.

The moment she was away from the lighted windows of the house, the night seemed very black. The fog had thinned, however, and most of it had drifted away, so that lights were visible on distant hills. But there were no stars showing in the sky, and no lights nearby. There was a pond out there, she knew, but she couldn't see it now. The woods were just beyond the garage—she'd had a glimpse of stark, bare trees while the moving men were here. There were a hundred acres of those woods which belonged to the Seale property—the Forster property—and climbed the mountain behind the house. That was one of the big appeals of this place for Dad—all that wooded mountain. But now she could sense the forest, black and impenetrable and strange, crowding all around like a high black wall, with no streetlights shining through, no bright city windows—only that flat wall of blackness.

Surely there would be lights somewhere near if she went down to the road. It was only a winding dirt lane leading through more trees, but there were people who lived along it. Hemlock Road, it was called. She could just make out the curving turn of the steep driveway, and she followed it downward, now and then looking back at the windows of the Seale house for reassurance. *The Seale house.* She wondered if it would ever be the Forster house to her.

The quiet was almost the worst thing of all. No traffic sounds, no auto horns, no clashing of machinery. The city roared all the time, though when you lived there you hardly noticed the noise it made. Perhaps people who lived in the country didn't notice the silence that seemed to pulse in Sandy's ears. Such utter quiet did not seem natural to her, and it was a little frightening. As if she might be the only person left in this dark, quiet world.

She followed the driveway down to the place where it joined the road, and stepped out into rutted dirt tracks. More trees crowded close on the opposite side, with only their skeletal branches outlined against a faintly lighter sky. Toward the highway in the direction of the Wendel house, she could see nothing. The road took a turn down there that blocked their house from view. But when she looked the other way she could see the old stone house where Sam and Lucy Haines lived with their granddaughter, Trina.

Yes, there were lights down there, and her heart quickened with an unexpected feeling of pleasure. The bright windows looked warm and inviting, shining out of the darkness. Tomorrow she would meet Trina Carpozi. And never mind what Melissa Morris thought of her. The things Mrs. Morris had said about Trina returned to Sandy, and she considered them with sympathy. Imagine how awful it would be not to have a mother and father. A girl like that would need a friend. She wouldn't be snooty like Melissa Morris.

Something crackled in the woods across the road, and Sandy whirled about, staring all around, trying to force herself to see through the blackness, aware of some hidden danger. The rustling came again, and she fled as though she might be pursued, running breathlessly up the drive toward the lighted house and the safety of her own mother's and father's company.

The country had a frightening life of its own that she didn't understand. She wasn't sure she could ever get used to it.

2

Encounter on the Mountain

In spite of the disorder of both her room and her emotions, Sandy slept well that night, with only a few uneasy dreams. She awakened to the sounds of Dad moving furniture around and Mother banging pans in the kitchen. From where she lay in bed she could look out the nearest window at the forest growing up a steep brown hillside behind the house. Near her windows was a grove of leaning birch trees, their trunks white against the rest of the brown woods. Only a few evergreens showed color in that endless marching of dead branches. Perhaps this was the dullest time of year, with the autumn colors gone and the snow yet to come.

The house had its back to the east, so the sun rose behind the mountain and it would be later in the morning before it topped the trees. But at least there was morning light out there, and Sandy felt less gloomy and discouraged than she had the night before. After all, there were interesting things to look forward to today. Perhaps she would meet Trina and Cliff. And perhaps she could drive in to Halcyon with her father when he went to the Morris Hardware Store.

Anticipation prompted her to action, and she slid out of bed and hurried through the bathroom. When she had dressed in jeans and a yellow sweater, she went into the living room, where her father had rolled down the beige rug and placed some of the furniture where Mother wanted it to go. But she hardly saw the room because the double picture windows drew her with their dramatic display.

There was no fog this morning and she could see the wide panorama of blue sky and long distant mountain that ran like a straight ruled line across the horizon. She had seen a snapshot of this, and she knew it was called the Blue Mountain. Though she liked the Indian name best— the Kittatinny range, or the Endless Hills. Part of the mountain was across the Delaware River in Pennyslvania, the rest in New Jersey. The huge cleft of the Delaware Water Gap broke the range into two precipitous cliffs and let the river pour through, marking the boundary between the two states.

When she had looked long enough, she ran through the living room and dining room, waving to her father, who was setting up the dining room table, hurrying out to the kitchen. Mother must have been up early, because most of the kitchen things were unpacked and put away in cupboards. Their own mountain wasn't so high behind this end of the house, and a glinting of sun showed through treetops, touching the windows over the sink. Now she could see the triangular pond beyond the driveway and lawn, its water a pale, shining green in the morning light. She knew it was an artificial pond which Mr. Seale had built last summer. One bank of it was a dam which held the water in. It would be wonderful for swimming when warm weather came, and perhaps for skating in the winter.

Mother kissed her good morning, looking more like her cheerful self. Sandy found she was enormously hungry and ate breakfast with a good appetite. Dad had finished his meal earlier, but he came out to sit at the table and have another cup of coffee while Sandy ate.

"I'm going in to Halcyon around ten thirty," he told her. "You can come along if you like. Your mother wants to stay here and go on with her unpacking. I won't put in a full day at the store until Monday, since there's so much to do here. But I want to have a look around and get better acquainted with Mrs. Morris. Perhaps you can see Melissa again. I hope you'll like her."

Sandy raised her shoulders, grimacing.

"What does that mean?" Dad asked.

"I don't know her," Sandy said. "I don't think she likes me."

"It takes a little time with new friends," Mother put in, busy at the sink with the frying pan.

"Mm," Dad said. "Anyway, I hope you'll make an effort here, Sandy. I want things to go well between Mrs. Morris and me, since we're partners. If you and Melissa get along, it will make everything that much more comfortable. That's important for all of us, you know."

It was Sandy's turn to say, "Mm." She didn't really

know how she could be friends with Melissa Morris if Melissa didn't want her for a friend. But she was willing to try to please Dad. Even though he had wanted to move to the country, she knew everything wasn't going to be easy for him right away.

After breakfast, she helped Mother put the dishes into the washer, and then went to work straightening out her own room and unpacking some of her own possessions. But the outdoors seemed to be calling her urgently, with a whole new world to explore out there. So when she felt she had made enough headway with her tasks, she asked if she might go outside.

"There's a trail you can see from the kitchen windows," she said to Mother. "Out there beside the pond. It leads up into the woods, and perhaps I could follow it a little way."

"Of course," Mother said. "I'm eager to go up there myself, but I want to finish a few more things in the house first, while Dad's around to help. Mr. Seale told us he had cut several trails and cross trails through the woods. They're wide enough to take the snowmobile he sold us— later on, when there's snow."

That promised to be fun, Sandy thought. Dad had done a little snowmobiling back in New York when they'd visited friends out of town in winter.

"Just watch your turns," Mother added, "and stay on the trails. You can get lost up there, until you know your way around."

The morning was bright and warm for December, and once more a sweater was all she needed. She ran across the intervening grass that was still green and untouched by winter. At the edge of the forest the trail led upward, curving quickly out of sight. As she followed it trees shut her in, cutting her off from the house, so that when she looked back it had vanished behind the forest wall. The woods seemed still and deep, brown-dark in their recesses, but she was no longer afraid as she had been last night. After all, there was nothing here to hurt her, and the morning was not as mysteriously silent as the night had seemed.

A few chickadees followed her route, hopping along branches high overhead, then flying on to another tree to watch her approach with bright-eyed interest. The little black-capped birds gave her a feeling of nearby friendliness, and their chirpings broke the silence. The path

wound upward, brown with dead leaves, and snagged here
and there with the rough roots of trees. It hadn't been cold
enough for the ground to freeze solid, and it was a little
soggy at times, as though there were nearby springs, and
in one place a narrow watercourse twisted its way down
the hill. In a sky far bluer than any she had seen in the
city, a jet plane flew over—only a silver speck in all that
blue—yet with a faraway roaring that reminded her of cities and the great airport from which it had come.

The path took another winding turn, and Sandy's sense
of direction grew confused. She was no longer sure which
way the house lay. But it didn't matter. She had only to
follow the path downhill and she would find her way
again.

On her left a grove of tall hemlock trees became visible
across an opening in the woods, following a straight line,
as though someone must have planted them there a long
time ago. Between the grove and the trail she followed, a
field of reddish earth as big as a city block spread out in a
great raw patch where nothing grew—not even weeds. She
wondered about it as she walked on. Why had so large an
expanse been cleared of trees and left bare?

Beside the road, a wall of piled-up stones ran for a little
way, and then turned off among the trees, marking some
long-forgotten boundary. She wondered if people had once
lived up here in this forest. Certainly the wall had been
built by human hands, though it looked old and crum-
bling. Perhaps there had once been farming land and pas-
tures up here, long since abandoned and given back to wil-
derness.

On the opposite side of the road from the wall rose a
great mass of gray rock, filled with crevices and rough toe-
holds. It would be fun to climb that sometime, Sandy
thought, but at the moment she was more interested in the
tall hemlock trees that looked so beautifully green in the
heart of these dead winter woods. As she looked at them
something moved—and a remarkable thing happened.

Out from among the hemlocks stepped a brown doe and
two fawns. Sandy stood very still, holding her breath. The
mother deer looked at her with gentle, unfrightened eyes
and stood as still as Sandy. She was not alarmed, but she
was watching, waiting to see what sort of creature Sandy
was, what she might do. One of the half-grown fawns was

even more interested and took several steps in her direction before it too stopped to stare fixedly.

But Sandy could not keep as still as these wild things. In a few moments she had to move. At once the mother deer leaped away, the underside of her tail showing white as she took flight. The two fawns flung up their tails and followed their mother, so that three white flags seemed to wave among the brush before they disappeared from sight. In a moment the woods were empty of life except for a small chipmunk which came out from among the rocks of the wall and scurried along the top, busy with its own affairs on this warm and springlike day.

With a long, released sigh Sandy moved on up the trail. She knew she had witnessed something wonderful—something not one other friend of hers had ever seen outside a zoo. The country had its rewards after all, and she found that she walked with a quickened step and an increased interest in all that lay around her.

On a tree ahead someone had tacked a red sign, printed in black with the words No HUNTING. Sandy thought of hunters chasing those beautiful deer, and she was glad they would not be allowed in these woods.

She walked along slowly, feeling at peace—yet when something rustled in the brush and she heard the crackling of a twig under an unseen foot, she experienced a return of her last night's uneasiness. The woods were still strange, and she was not sure of what they might hide. When the crackling continued she halted on the path, her heart thumping, ready for flight if some unknown danger threatened.

But there was no danger. From around a turn in the uphill path a girl and a dog came into sight. The girl must have been about Sandy's age, or a little older. She was certainly bigger, and her appearance was not particularly attractive. She had short hair the color of a dead leaf—rather untidy hair that looked as if she had not bothered to comb it this morning. Her face was round and expressionless, and her odd, greenish eyes stared at Sandy with the same fixed, unblinking look the doe had shown. She wore patched blue jeans, a faded pink blouse with a torn sleeve, and her body seemed lumpish and a little too fat.

The dog was equally nondescript. It was a scrawny brown-and-white mongrel, and it walked with a limp be-

cause its left hind leg was crooked. Both girl and dog
came toward Sandy with watchful caution.

The dog spoke first. He bounded suddenly toward
Sandy with his lopsided gait, barking furiously and snapping at her ankles. Sandy backed away, and after too long
a moment the girl called to her dog.

"Come back here, Charlie, come back! Lie down, boy!"

A little to Sandy's surprise, and certainly to her relief,
the mongrel returned to his owner and sat down at her
feet, his brown eyes looking up at her in loving obedience.

The girl's stare was even less friendly than the dog's approach, and as she came toward Sandy, she spoke in a
rough, unpleasant voice.

"Who are you? What are you doing in these woods?"

Sandy found herself bristling. "I'm Sandy Forster, and
these are my father's woods. Our woods."

The other girl came closer, and Charlie came with her.
The blank expression did not change, and she seemed
unimpressed by Sandy's words.

"Mr. Seale says woods should belong to everyone. He
says men can only be guardians of them. So how can the
woods belong to you?"

Sandy had supposed that when someone bought a piece
of land, he owned that land, but she did not want to argue
with this unpleasant girl.

"Are you Trina Carpozi?" she asked.

"What if I am? What's it to you?"

This was certainly no approach to friendship, and by
this time Sandy had decided that she didn't want this girl
for a friend anyway. Now she could cross two people off
her hopeful list—Melissa and Trina. That left only one
other young person in the neighborhood—the boy, Cliff
Wendel. If he was impossible, she would be totally without
friends.

The thought was discouraging, but she tilted her chin
slightly to show Trina she was unintimidated by anything
she had said, and started to walk past her up the trail. At
once Trina thrust out an arm and stopped her, while Charlie uttered a warning bark.

"Don't go up there!" Trina said.

Sandy sidestepped the thrusting arm. "Why shouldn't I?
This is my father's land."

"It's dangerous up there." Trina's green eyes stared at

her without blinking. "If you go up there, you can get hurt."

"I don't believe you," Sandy said, and continued her way up the trail.

Trina came after her, moving rather awkwardly as though she had trouble with her feet. This time she caught Sandy by the arm and swung her about with no uncertain strength.

"There's a bear in the woods up there. And if you've got any sense, you won't go anywhere near a bear."

"A bear?" Sandy said, believing none of this. "Don't be silly. This is New Jersey, not the Wild West."

"Okay," the girl said. "Don't say I didn't tell you," and she let go of Sandy's arm and turned back to the downhill trail. She still moved awkwardly, as though she could not walk so fast as she'd have liked, and there was a twist to one foot. The brown-and-white mongrel, who had trouble with his own feet, hurried after her. In a moment they were around a turn and out of sight.

Sandy stared after the two in astonishment. Why in the world had Trina treated her so unpleasantly? Why had she tried to frighten her with that story of a bear? In any case Sandy did not mean to be frightened, and she started up the path again. Not for a minute did she believe in the presence of a bear.

The trail steepened, climbing the rise of a small hill to vanish over its rim. There were no distant views to be seen because of the trees that crowded in thickly on all sides. Everything was quiet again, since the chickadees had chosen to follow Trina down the mountain. Nevertheless, Sandy walked on boldly, climbing the hill. When she reached the ridge the trail fell away again, dipping into a gloomy hollow in the heart of the mountain. Here the trees were old and tall and there were no stone walls to mark the interference of man. The sky seemed darkened by their reaching branches, and the mountain was utterly still. Yet human beings had been here.

As she went a few steps down toward the hollow, she saw a small gray log cabin that looked almost like part of the forest, with its stone chimney and rough bark sides. Once more she stood staring, delighted by this unexpected discovery. How wonderful to find this little house here in the woods. All sorts of possibilities suggested themselves, and she wondered if her father and mother knew of the cabin's existence. This would make a wonderful place for picnicking or camping out. If there really was a bear, she would only need to run inside and shut the door.

As she neared the cabin, she saw that a stone fireplace had been built for outdoor cookouts. So it would be possible to camp here in the cabin.

Eagerly she moved toward the door—and at that moment something exploded into the air practically in her face. With a great drumming and whirring, a big brown bird brushed past her as it took flight in a steep climb and flew off into the woods. It had been so nearly the color of brown winter brush that she had not seen it, and the sudden explosion of sound and movement at her very feet frightened her badly. She stepped back, her heart pounding, and suddenly the woods all around seemed as alarmingly mysterious as they had last night. A little way off, more rustling and crackling sounded in the undergrowth, but she did not wait to see whether it was a deer—or a bear. She tore heedlessly along the trail, wanting only to get home. A protruding root tripped her as she ran, and she sprawled on the path. At least her jeans saved her from skinning a knee.

After that she ran more cautiously, but she still hurried and she did not look back, lest she find that some horror was chasing her down the path through the dark woods.

By the time Sandy reached the edge of the trees, Trina Carpozi was nowhere in sight. She rushed out onto the green lawn and came to a halt, feeling a little foolish, now that she was safely home and the house stood before her in the warming sunshine looking normal and everyday.

For the first time she thought of what an attractive house it was, with white clapboard sides and pointed eaves painted a dark red. Grass spread on a level all around, separating the house from the woods, and in front the lawn dipped steeply down to the road. In that direction, off above the treetops, the Delaware Water Gap split the level blue range of mountains.

When she had caught her breath, Sandy walked more slowly across the grass and went in the front door, to meet her father coming along the hall. He had changed to country clothes—a red-checked wool shirt, brown corduroy pants, and a red, billed cap.

"Hello," he said. "I was wondering if you'd get back in

time. I'm ready to drive in to town. If you want to come along. tell your mother we're leaving."

Sandy dashed into the living room, where her mother was hanging pictures. Jenny Forster gazed at her daughter with perceptive eyes.

"What's the matter? You look as though you'd had a fright."

She had thought she was perfectly cool by the time she entered the house, but her mother had seen through that pose, and Sandy laughed ruefully.

"It was just that a dumb old bird flew up in my face and scared me."

Her mother laughed. "A grouse, probably. One did that to us when we went up in the woods with Mr. Seale."

"Did you know there's a cabin up there?"

"Yes—he showed it to us. We thought we'd let you find it for yourself and have the fun of a surprise. Did you go inside?"

"Not yet." Sandy said nothing about Trina and her warnings of a bear. With Dad waiting, there wasn't time to go into all that.

From outside, her father's voice shouted her name, and Sandy hurried to announce that she was going in to town with Dad. Mother gave her a hasty brushing down to remove leaves from her jeans, and smoothed her hair with a quick hand.

"All right—run along."

Dad had the car out and Sandy tumbled into the seat beside him. He wasn't the most patient man in the world, and it didn't do to keep him waiting too long. They followed the long curve of the driveway down to the road.

"I hope Seale was righᵗ about the snow-removing equipment working well," Dad said. "I'd hate to be snowed in on that drive."

But there was no snow to worry about yet, and the trip down the mountain on the main highway was a pleasant one. Views of the valley spread out far below on the left-hand side of the road, while the wooded mountain wall rose to still greater heights on the right.

They drove in to Halcyon across a stone bridge spanning a stream that tumbled over rocks and followed a winding course down the valley. Several old stone houses were clustered near the center of the village, giving it a peaceful, old-fashioned flavor.

Sandy knew that Moravians had settled here two hundred years ago. They were a religious group from Europe that had been persecuted in their native land in the 1700's. Many of them settled in New Jersey and Pennsylvania. Halcyon meant something quiet and peaceful, and this little village, dreaming in the December sunshine, had that look of peace to Sandy's city-bred eyes. Perhaps a little too much peace and harmony, but restful, at least after her unsettling encounters on the mountain.

The Morris Hardware Store was on Main Street, wedged between a grocery store and a bank. Out behind was a vacant lot where trucks could unload, and when Dad had parked his car there they got out and went into the store. Apparently Mrs. Morris sold a little of everything, and well-stocked shelves ran along every wall, while tables with aisles down either side were piled with everything from kitchenware to cans of paint.

Sandy looked around in dismay. This was quite evidently a country store, and not at all like the bright, clean, modern advertising offices where Dad had worked in New York. The store was deep and narrow and high-ceilinged, with a faintly dusty, metallic odor that was probably due to very little outside ventilation. Mrs. Morris sat behind a desk enclosure, studying an account book, while a gangly boy in his late teens waited on a customer. When she saw Dad and Sandy, she stood up to welcome them with that same rather anxious expression she had worn when she visited the house last night. This morning her plump person was clothed in a navy skirt and green cardigan sweater.

"Good morning," Dad said. "Jenny wanted me to tell you how much we enjoyed that casserole last night. Now I've come to get acquainted with the store. At least, to begin. On Monday I'll come in full time."

"That's fine," Mrs. Morris said. "I expect you'll want to start learning the stock, so you'll know where everything is." She regarded Sandy doubtfully. "This will be tiresome for you. Why don't you go down the road to where Melissa is visiting a friend? I'm sure they'll be glad to see you, and . . . uh . . ." she broke off, as though she was not so sure of this as she wanted to be.

Dad took her up at once. "A good idea. Can you show Sandy the house so she can find her way? Then she can wait there until I pick her up."

"I don't mind staying in the store—" Sandy began, but no one seemed to hear her. Mrs. Morris was already at the door, gesturing down the street.

"There you are. That green house across the highway. The one with the brown shingled roof. That's where Debra Elliot lives. Run on down and ring the bell. Tell them I sent you." She patted Sandy on the shoulder and gave her a little push out the door.

Sandy found herself on the sidewalk, with occasional traffic running past on the highway that cut directly through the village. She had no desire to barge in on Melissa and her friend, but there seemed nothing else to do but walk down the street. She passed another stone house and studied it with an interest that served to delay her progress. It was built squarely, with a sloping roof and windows set in geometric balance on either side of a central door.

But she couldn't stand around studying old stone forever, so she crossed the highway between cars and walked reluctantly toward the green house. On the porch she paused, still wishing for some way to escape what she had to do. As she hesitated, a tall woman with fluffy brown hair and a cheerful smile came to open the door.

"Hello," the woman said. "Are you looking for someone?"

Sandy explained who she was, and that Mrs. Morris had sent her over. At once Mrs. Elliot invited her in.

"The girls are in the living room playing Monopoly. Go right in. They'll be glad to see you. I've got a pan on the stove, so I have to run."

Once more Sandy found that she had been thrust toward something she didn't want to do. She could hear voices coming from the doorway off the hall, and she walked slowly toward the sound. When she reached the open door she paused hesitantly, looking into the room.

3

A Broken Flowerpot

Three girls sat on the floor, their heads bent over a Monopoly board. One of them was Melissa. Her short, fair hair shone in the sunlight from a window as she moved a counter in the direction of Park Place. The other two girls were about the same age, one with brown hair tied into two ponytails, the other with short, straight black hair. On the wide windowsill a gray tabby cat lay sleeping in the sun.

Sandy must have made some sound, for the girls raised their heads and stared toward the door. It was hard to face three strange girls when she was the newcomer. There was no smile of welcome on any of the three faces—just a waiting curiosity. Sandy made herself speak.

"Hello, Melissa. Mrs. Elliot said to come in. My father's over at the store with your mother."

Melissa looked the least welcoming of all, but she managed a grudging, "Hello," and made no other response.

The girl with the two ponytails scrambled to her feet, smiling in a more friendly fashion. "You must be Sandy Forster. I'm Debra Elliot, and this is Ginger Santesen. Come on in." Debra had a snub nose with plentiful freckles across it, and a wide, cheerful mouth. This was a girl she might like, Sandy thought as she walked reluctantly into the room. At least Debra was willing to play hostess.

Melissa said, "We're in the middle of a game."

"I can watch," Sandy told her.

She did not sit on the floor beside the others, but curled herself into a comfortable worn armchair near a window. At once the gray cat rose from the sill and sprang into her lap. Its warm body was comforting, and Sandy stroked its fur listening to the loud purring. The cat, at least, had welcomed her.

The three went back to their game, with varied cries of triumph and despair, and some good-natured wrangling

29

among themselves. They seemed to have forgotten Sandy,
until Melissa turned suddenly in her direction.

"Have you seen Trina Carpozi yet?" she asked.

"I saw her this morning," Sandy admitted. "She was up
in the woods with her dog."

"Charlie!" Melissa said, and the other two girls laughed.

"Such a silly name for a dog!" Ginger, the black-haired
girl, made a derisive, impudent face.

"She named it after her father," Melissa said. "Can you
imagine naming a dog after your father?"

Ginger looked astonished. "I didn't know that. Why did
she?"

"Because she's weird," Debra said. "I heard Mom telling
Dad that her father ran off and left Trina and her mother
when Trina was only six. So you wouldn't think she'd
name anything after him."

Melissa was watching Sandy. "What did she say when
you met her?"

"She—wasn't very friendly. She told me to get out of
the woods."

"But they're your woods," Debra said, pulling at one of
her brown ponytails.

"She thinks they're hers," Melissa explained. "That's because Mr. Seale used to let her roam all through them.
Anyway—wait till Monday!"

Debra and Ginger looked at Melissa knowingly, and the
three began to laugh as though something enormously
funny had been said.

Sandy was immediately curious. "What will happen on
Monday?"

The three seemed to find this even funnier and they
laughed until they choked and tears came into Ginger's
eyes—tears of mirth. The entire performance left Sandy
both bewildered and uncomfortable, and her blank expression seemed to amuse the girls even more. They
looked at her and then at each other, and doubled over
with laughter.

Sandy began to feel annoyed. "If there's a joke, you
might tell me."

"The joke is Trina Carpozi," Melissa said, and ceased
her laughter as if a switch had been turned off.

After a few more choking gurgles, the other two
stopped laughing as well, watching Melissa as though they
waited for her lead. The sudden silence seemed more dis-

turbing than the laughter. Something was going on here that Sandy did not understand, and she didn't like the feeling of it. Something was wrong, but she couldn't figure out what it was.

Debra, who seemed the friendliest of the three, broke the silence. "Will you start school on Monday?" she asked Sandy.

"I suppose so," Sandy said.

"Then you'll probably be in our room—Mr. Wendel's room. He's pretty nice, even though he's a new teacher. We have fun in his room. But you'll have to be careful about dumb old Trina."

"Careful?" Sandy was bewildered.

Debra gave her ponytail another tug. "I mean Mr. Wendel won't stand for anything. If you come in with us, you'll have to help keep him from catching on."

"Catching on to what?" Sandy felt more lost than ever.

Debra was about to explain, but Melissa reached over and poked her. "I didn't say she was coming in with us."

"But since her father's going to be a partner in your mother's store," Debra began, only to have Melissa frown at her.

"It's still *my* father's store!" Melissa snapped.

But Melissa's father was dead—a year or so ago, Sandy thought, and suddenly began to understand Melissa a little. She still wanted it to be *her* father's store, and she might very well resent having Ted Forster come in and take over. In which case, she might resent his daughter as well.

The three girls returned their attention to the Monopoly board, and paid no attention to Sandy for a long while. The cat went to sleep in her lap, and the minutes ticked slowly, endlessly by. This wasn't any fun at all, and increasingly Sandy wished herself elsewhere. It would have been more interesting in the store, even if she had nothing to look at but paint and nails. Monopoly was such a long game when you could only watch.

When she was sure her legs were going to sleep, along with the cat, she shoved the gray tabby off her lap and stood up. Then she went to the window and looked out at the highway. There was nothing interesting out there either and she decided to startle these girls into paying some attention to her.

"Are there bears in the woods around here?" she asked.

All three stared at her, and Ginger giggled.

"Trina said there was a bear in our woods," Sandy went on.

"She likes to scare people." Melissa turned back to the game, nudging Ginger. "It's your turn."

"There was something in the Blairstown paper about a woman near Stillwater who was putting out her garbage one morning and saw a bear," Debra offered.

Melissa only shrugged. "People are always seeing things. Hurry up, Ginger."

They had forgotten Sandy again, and she moved restlessly about the room. After a little while, she tried again to break in.

"I expect I'll see Mr. Wendel before Monday," she remarked. "Mother said he might drop in during this weekend. So then I can ask him about Trina. If you don't want to tell me what's so funny about her, perhaps he will."

She had their attention at once. The three looked up from their game with varying questions and doubts in their eyes.

Melissa spoke quietly, reasonably. "You don't want Trina for a friend, Sandy."

"I don't think she wants me for a friend," Sandy said.

"Of course she doesn't. Who does she care about? She's rough and mean and you never know what she'll do next. In school she's dumb as anything. Mr. Wendel thinks he can help her, but our last teacher knew it was hopeless. She even had the psychiatrist talk to her. And somebody's always going out to see her grandparents."

"That's not very funny," Sandy said. "I don't see why you were laughing."

Unexpectedly, Melissa seemed more friendly than before. She actually smiled at Sandy, though her blue eyes still held a cool and critical look.

"Wait until Monday and you'll understand better. For now, we can give you some Monopoly money and let you into our game if you want to play. That's okay, isn't it, girls?"

The other two seemed as surprised by this turnabout as Sandy, but they moved apart so she could sit between them at the board. She was not altogether sure she wanted to get into the game by this time, or if she liked any of these girls—but it was a change to be included, instead of shut out. She sat cross-legged on the floor between Debra and Ginger, and gave her attention to the game. She couldn't catch up with the others, but at least this was something to do that was better than watching. Between moves, however, she continued to consider the three girls.

Clearly Melissa was the leader whom Ginger and Debra listened to about most things, and Melissa, for some reason. had suddenly decided to be friendly. Perhaps because Sandy had mentioned questioning Mr. Wendel and Melissa did not want that. Or perhaps it was just a matter of letting the other girls get used to her, of waiting a little while for them to accept her. At least there was no more uncomfortable talk about Trina, and by the time her father came to pick her up and take her home for lunch, Sandy felt more hopeful about school on Monday. Everything was working out after all, and she would not have to walk, a complete stranger, into a strange schoolroom.

The girls jumped up and came to the door with her when she left, and Melissa was pleasant and friendly. Nevertheless, Sandy did not look back as she walked out to the car, for fear she might find the three laughing again—this time at her.

"Well, I see you're beginning to make friends," Dad said as they drove through town toward home.

"I guess so." Sandy was not entirely sure.

On the way up the mountain Dad began to talk about his morning at the store. He sounded more cheerful about counting nails, or whatever he had been doing, than he'd ever been about writing ads for soap flakes.

"I think it's going to turn out well," he told Sandy, talking to her as if she were grown-up, as he sometimes did. "Mrs. Morris not only needs someone to take over the handling of heavy items but she also needs someone in the business end. Apparently she leaned on her husband in such matters, and now I can begin to take them over. It's interesting, though, how many more women are coming into the hardware business these days than used to in the past."

"Mother says women can do anything, if you give them a chance," Sandy said.

Dad nodded. "I know. That's why she left all the heavy furniture-moving for me."

They laughed together. Sandy rather enjoyed the Women's Lib arguments that went on between Mother and Dad these days. No one seemed to win, one way or the other, but Mother said it was healthy to talk about such things and not try to put females into just one category. Not that Mother wanted to be a career woman. It was just that she felt she had the right to be if that was what she wished.

When questions were asked about Sandy's morning, she managed to be vague and general. She said nothing about Trina's behavior on the mountain, or about the way Melissa and her friends had seemed to find Trina a subject for their laughter. She had decided it would be better to wait until school on Monday, when she could watch those three and see if she could find out what was going on.

After lunch there was more unpacking to be done, more empty cartons to be carried out to the garage, and the house began to take on a lived-in look. When the doorbell rang and Sandy went to answer it, she found Mr. Wendel and his son, Cliff, on the porch.

Frank Wendel had reddish hair that was thinning a little on top, and his eyes were distorted behind the thick lenses of his glasses. He was thin and rather small—not very impressive in appearance. If this was to be her teacher, Sandy felt disappointed. Cliff, on the other hand, had fiery-red hair and was almost as tall as his father, and a lot huskier.

Sandy invited them in, and Mother and Dad came to shake hands. By this time there was enough furniture set around the living room so that it was possible to invite company into it, and the Wendels sat down and admired the magnificent view.

"We're in a hollow down the road," Mr. Wendel said, "and can't see as far into the distance as you can up here. We like the feeling of trees all around, and we enjoy living in this area. Betty wanted me to ask you all down for supper tomorrow night. Since we've moved in recently ourselves, we know how awkward cooking can be for a few days until you get sorted out."

Mother accepted with pleasure. As Mr. Wendel talked, Sandy watched and wondered about him. Wondered what he would be like in a classroom. He seemed pleasant and at least he didn't embarrass her by fixing his attention upon her and talking to her like a new pupil.

When there was a break in the conversation, Cliff stood up. "I told Trina Carpozi I'd bring her some birdseed from town, so maybe I'd better go down there."

"Sure," Mr. Wendel said. Then he turned to Sandy. "Have you met Trina yet?"

Sandy nodded without explaining.

Perhaps Mr. Wendel understood her silence, for he pressed her no farther. "Cliff, why don't you take Sandy with you down to Trina's? That's an interesting old house her grandparents own. She might like to see it."

"Come along if you want to," Cliff said, and Sandy was glad to go with him and get better acquainted.

He stopped to take a sack of birdseed out of the back of his father's station wagon before they started down the drive.

As they walked down to the road together, she found Cliff easy to talk to. She had no feeling that he was holding back, or being critical of her as Melissa had been.

When he said, "What did you think of Trina when you met her?" she found herself glad to answer him. She wanted to talk to someone about Trina.

He did not seem surprised about what had happened in the woods. "Trina's had a lot of trouble in her life, and she hated it when the Seales moved away and we knew you were coming. I think she's—well—scared about a lot of things."

Trina had not seemed scared about anything to Sandy, but now that she was to meet her again, she felt curious about the girl, and all the more interested in knowing what Melissa and her friends seemed to be plotting against her.

The house where Sam and Lucy Haines lived was two hundred years old, and the stones had weathered to a pink-ish-yellow color that seemed to glow in the setting of dead-brown trees. Long ago a white porch had been built onto the front of the square Moravian house, and now its paint was cracked and peeling. Out at the side of the house an old man was cutting up a tree for firewood, using a chain saw. The high, whining buzz cut off the sound of their approach, and he did not look around.

Cliff waited until the saw had bitten through the trunk and the old man had switched it off. Then he said, "Hi, Mr. Haines. This is Sandy Forster, who's come to live in the Seale house."

Under the green-and-white checked shirt and baggy gray pants, the old man's body seemed shapeless, as though it had long since sagged away from the outlines of youth. He was partially bald, and a rim of gray hair

ringed his scalp. His eyes were a pale, faded blue and the
rims encased them in wrinkles. Nevertheless, they were
eyes that looked at Sandy in a lively, searching way, as
though he asked questions she did not know how to answer.

"Hi," he said to them both. And to Cliff, "You looking
for Trina?"

Cliff nodded. "I've brought her some birdseed." He set
the sack down on the ground.

"She's in the house." Mr. Haines sighed. "She's been upset as all get-out lately, so go easy. She's got her grandmother running up the walls, Lucy's that nervous over
Trina. I don't know if—"

Sandy sensed that he was about to send them away, but
Cliff moved confidently toward the house. "We'll look for
her. Come along, Sandy."

The old man watched them go, offering no further ob-
jection, and Cliff led the way up to the porch. He knocked
on the door and called out Trina's name. But it was
Trina's grandmother who opened the door. At the same
instant the yapping little mongrel Sandy had seen in the
woods came dashing at the visitors, and Mrs. Haines
thrust him away with one foot.

"Shut up—you! Get back there! Lie down!"

Charlie, who had obeyed Trina very well, paid no attention to her grandmother. He ducked her foot and made a
dash for Cliff. The red-haired boy leaned over and cheerfully scooped him up in his arms. Charlie stopped yapping
and tried to lather Cliff's face with an affectionate pink
tongue.

"He's all right," Cliff assured Mrs. Haines. "It's just that
he's a good watchdog and guardian. Is Trina around?"

"She's around," Mrs. Haines said and stepped somewhat
reluctantly back from the door to let them in. She was a
tall, rather gaunt woman with thinning gray hair pulled
into a bun at the back of her head. Her eyes were nearly
black, and, like her thin hands, they seemed to move all
the time. They darted nervous looks here and there, never
resting long on any one thing, glancing at Sandy, looking
quickly away, then back again. And while her hands and
her eyes moved restlessly, her tongue moved too. She
never seemed to stop talking, engulfing her visitors in a
torrent of words.

Feeling embarrassed by this vocal stream, Sandy stood

in the doorway and looked about the small, old-fashioned room. It was spotlessly clean and neat. There were doilies on the tables, and under the lamps. White lace antimacassars graced the back of every upholstered chair. The red-figured rug was worn and faded, but the muslin curtains at the windows looked new and fresh. On the mantel, and everywhere else that there was space, small ornaments were crowded—china dogs and cats, several seashells and polished stones, a plastic shepherdess in a blue hat. On the walls were framed pictures—to Sandy's eyes all rather old-fashioned and stiff. But the most overpowering thing about the room was the collection of plants. Flowerpots lined every windowsill. Geraniums and African violets were in bloom. Philodendron overflowed its container and reached toward the floor. Quite evidently, Mrs. Haines had a green thumb.

While Sandy looked around, the old woman talked on and on. "So you're the girl who's come to live in the Seale house? Come in, come in and shut the door. It's getting colder outside every day. And the cold absolutely kills my poor back. I couldn't sleep a wink all night long for the aching. Cliff, Sam says you're coming along well with that tray you're making for your mother out in the workshop. It's a good thing Sam likes all that woodworking. Gives him something to do. Don't know how he'd make out if it wasn't for his workshop. Nothing to do here in the country. Nobody to see. And at night I can't sleep because of my back."

Cliff seemed accustomed to this rush of words, and knew that no response was expected of him. He walked to a table in the center of the room and gestured toward a photograph in a plastic frame.

"Sandy, that's Trina's mother. Wasn't she pretty?"

Mrs. Haines, distracted from a fresh account of her aches and pains, flew into more words about her daughter. "Pretty! Della was a real beauty, Cliff. She could have gone into the movies any day. Why she ever wanted to work in that diner, I couldn't see. If she hadn't worked in that awful place, she'd never have met that good-for-nothing Charlie Carpozi. This picture was taken when she was seventeen. Just two months before she ran off with him!"

Across the room, behind Sandy and Cliff, there was a sudden crash and they turned around. Trina, her short hair as untidy as ever, her eyes greenly alert, stood near the door to the hall. At her feet lay a broken flowerpot, the philodendron it had contained spreading its earth-encrusted roots and reaching tendrils along the floor. Black dirt had scattered across Mrs. Haines's carpet.

For a moment the old woman stood staring and speechless. Then she murmured, "Oh, wicked, wicked!" and ran to gather up strands of leafy philodendron as though she were rescuing a hurt child. Trina stepped aside disdainfully, one toe deliberately crunching earth into the carpet.

Cliff set Charlie down, and the little dog went leaping excitedly about the room, enjoying the sense of calamity, while Cliff knelt to help Mrs. Haines gather up the pieces of broken flowerpot. A scornful smile tugged at Trina's lips as she watched them for a moment. Then she turned to Sandy.

"What'd you come down here for?"

"Cliff brought me," Sandy said. She felt more shocked then affronted this time. Shocked by the way Mrs. Haines had talked, and by Trina's angry reaction in breaking the flowerpot. She knew very well that what had happened had been no accident.

Cliff looked up at Trina. "I got you that birdseed you wanted. It's outside."

Trina did not trouble to thank him, but looked again at Sandy with an air of defiance, as though she knew she was being criticized.

"My father was a swell person," she said. "I can remember him. He was smart and he had a real good education. *She*"—with a gesture toward the photograph of her mother—"only held him back because she was dumb. He had to leave her. He had to make his own life. He's a real famous artist now, and—"

Her grandmother almost spat out her words, flinging them at Trina. "Stop all that lying! You don't know anything about him, and you were too little when he went away to remember him. He's not an artist. He's not anything."

"You wouldn't know!" Trina said. She hurled herself out the front door into the sunny afternoon, and the door banged shut behind her.

Mrs. Haines dusted crumbs of earth from her hands and got up from her knees with difficulty. "I don't know what I'm going to do!" she wailed. "There's trouble at school, trouble at home. Two years and everything gets worse all the time. I never wanted her here. I'd never have taken her—but Sam said it was our duty. She probably caused Della's death—my poor baby had to work so hard to take care of herself and the child, too. So when she got the flu it went into pneumonia, and—"

"Maybe it's hard for Trina too," Cliff said gently.

"Hard? She makes it hard! She's not grateful for anything we do for her. She hasn't any friends. Nobody likes her. She doesn't want anybody to like her! It doesn't do any good for those people from school to come here to talk to me about her. There's nothing anybody can do with her. I'd be glad if they took her away to a children's home or somewhere—only Sam would have a fit."

Cliff signaled Sandy with his eyes, and they began to edge toward the door. "So long, Mrs. Haines," he said when they were close enough to make their escape and could slip outdoors.

Around the corner of the house the saw was still buzzing, and Cliff did not stop to speak to Mr. Haines. Trina was nowhere in sight. Sandy walked along the road beside Cliff, feeling horrified and a little sick.

"That was awful," she said as they started up the driveway to the house. Cliff nodded. His bright-red hair shone as cheerfully as ever in the sun, but he looked troubled and unhappy. "Everything seems wrong down there," Sandy went on. "Her grandmother shouldn't have talked about Trina's father like that, but Trina shouldn't be so mean and she shouldn't break her grandmother's things."

"I know," Cliff said.

"What's it like with her in school?"

"She doesn't want to work. She doesn't pay attention. She isn't interested in anything. She daydreams and acts dumb. Or else she bothers other people. Dad's worried about her. He'd like to help, but so far she won't let anybody get near her."

"Melissa Morris doesn't like her, does she?" Sandy asked.

Cliff snorted. "Melissa doesn't like anybody but Melissa!"

It was a relief to hear Cliff critical of Melissa Morris.

"Just the same, Melissa seems to have lots of friends," Sandy pointed out cautiously.

"Followers!" Cliff scoffed. "If you belong to that bunch, you have to do what Melissa says. You can have it!"

Sandy was not sure she wanted it, but she was eager to find out more from Cliff. More about school, more about Melissa and her friends. "What does your father think of Melissa?"

"Dad? Oh, he likes everybody. He's a born teacher, and he thinks there aren't any bad kids. But he doesn't always see things the way they look to the fellow in the next desk."

"You're not in the same room with Melissa and Trina, are you?"

"No—I'm a year ahead. But I know kids in their room and I've seen what goes on. I feel sorry for Trina. Maybe I even feel sorry for Melissa sometimes. One of these days things are going to catch up with her."

They had nearly reached the front door, and he stopped on the driveway and looked at Sandy.

"Say! Maybe you're the one who can make friends with Trina. She likes to wander around in your woods, and she'll need permission for that. So maybe you'll have a way to talk to her that nobody else has."

Sandy could only gaze at him in dismay. What she had seen at the Haines house had shaken and upset her. It certainly hadn't made her like Trina any better or feel any eagerness to seek her out again.

"I don't think so," she said as she and Cliff reached her house.

Mr. Wendel was getting ready to leave, and he and Mother and Dad were standing in the middle of the living room, talking. Sandy looked at them with a sudden new feeling—almost as though she had never seen her mother and father or this house before. A warm rush of love and gratitude went through her and she knew, more than ever, how lucky she was. How awful it would be not to have *her* mother and father, *her* home. How safe and free from ugliness it was here.

She went close, and Mother slipped an arm about her, giving Sandy a sense of being comforted. Now she could put Trina out of her mind. Trina was none of her business and she needn't think about her anymore. She had her own problems to solve.

4

The Hidden Box

It was Sunday afternoon, and the weather had turned cooler. The sky was still blue over the Gap, but a gray cloud bank seemed to be rising in the west.

The day had been an interesting one. In the morning they'd gone to church in Halcyon. Mrs. Morris and Melissa went to the same church, and so did Debra Elliot. So there was someone there whom the Forsters knew. Melissa and Debra greeted Sandy cheerfully, as though they had accepted her as their friend, and she felt reassured about her first day in school tomorrow.

On Saturday, Mother had done some shopping, so now the freezer was stocked, and they had a good Sunday dinner of roast chicken, finishing up with ice cream bought in town. Dad said he was going to get an old-fashioned ice-cream freezer one of these days and make real country ice cream—like the kind he'd had as a boy, and which Sandy had never tasted.

Of course there had been more unpacking, more straightening, more throwing out of junk they had somehow brought along when they should have left it behind. But now it was midafternoon and Sandy found herself free to roam the woods again. The day had turned breezy and the bare brown branches overhead thrashed in the wind, so that the forest seemed alive with sound. But at least it was identifiable sound, and Sandy did not mind it. She felt more comfortable in the woods by this time, more familiar with the trail she followed. In spite of the cooler weather, she did not need more than a sweater with her jeans.

She knew exactly where she was going, and she hoped she would not meet Trina Carpozi on the way this time. It hadn't been entirely easy for Sandy to put the girl out of her mind. Yesterday's happenings had made a deep and shocking impression, but she had held to her decision that the problem of Trina was not her problem. Even grown-ups were having trouble with her, and Cliff's suggestion that she try to make friends with her was too ridiculous to be considered.

Fortunately, the woods trails were empty, except for a few birds that chirped in the trees or complained about her as she went past, warning their fellows that an enemy was coming. Now and then Sandy found herself talking to them as she walked along, trying to assure them she meant no harm.

The log cabin seemed to come into view more quickly than before, now that she knew it was there, and she ran down the slope of hill toward the hollow below. Before she went inside the cabin, she circled the small house cautiously, making sure no one was about. There was not even a chipmunk to be seen, and she approached the door with a sense of anticipation. It was not locked and it opened readily at her touch. Feeling that she stepped into a kingdom of her own, she went through the door and closed it softly behind her.

The cabin consisted of one room, outlined by the log walls that enclosed it. Two bunks had been built along one wall—an upper and a lower—and there was a crude wooden table in the middle of the bare floor, with four rough-hewn chairs drawn up to it. On the table stood an old-fashioned oil lamp that had evidently been used, judging by its smoky chimney. The blackened stones of the fireplace waited for the next fire to be built, and there was an old bucket loaded with firewood on the hearth. Everything was clean and tidy, as though this had been a place Mr. Seale might have come to often and liked to keep in shape. Along one wall an unpainted cupboard held a few dishes, cups, and glasses, as well as some dented pans. There were jugs of water, and a small stock of canned and packaged foods, though one of the cereal packages looked as though some small animal had been gnawing at a corner.

Quite evidently, Mr. Seale had sometimes used this place to stay in overnight, and Sandy moved about, examining everything with growing pleasure. Perhaps she could persuade her mother and father to come up here and stay all night sometime. She was not sure this was something she would want to do alone. Anyway, it was wonderful to have a cabin of their own on their own property.

Having examined the interior of the cabin, Sandy turned her attention to the windows. These were unusual for so small a place. On three sides Mr. Seale had built small-scale picture windows, starting a little way above the floor, and reaching nearly to the low ceiling. They were windows that gave one a feeling of being outdoors. The woods and the grassy clearing at one side of the cabin seemed almost a part of the room, as if the outdoors were part of the furnishings. A bird feeder had been built near one window, and even as Sandy watched, a bright-red cardinal flew up to peck at the seed that had been left for him. This must have been what Trina wanted birdseed for.

Above the treetops Sandy could look up into branches that crisscrossed the sky. What a wonderful place this would be for watching the life of the forest. That, she suspected, was why it had been built. Mr. Seale was a naturalist, and he must have spent many hours here watching the animals and the birds.

When she returned her attention to the interior, she saw that a long drawer had been built in below the bottom bunk. It was probably to hold bedding, she thought, and went over to open it. The drawer stuck a little and jammed sideways, so she had to struggle with it for a moment to get it open. When she finally pulled it out, she saw that any blankets or bedding that might have been kept here had been removed, but there was a cardboard shoe box occupying the space. She wondered if this was something Mr. Seale had forgotten and left behind.

The box was not heavy, and the contents rattled about inside as she lifted it out and carried it to the table. When she took off the lid she found there was very little inside, and that little apparently worthless. But for a possible exception, the articles were strange for anyone to save. There was an old penknife which seemed to have rusted so badly that it would not open. There was a chipped glass bottle with a fancy stopper. The bottle was empty, but when Sandy pulled out the stopper she could catch a faint whiff of the sweet perfume the bottle must once have contained. The third object was a crude pincushion of the sort that a child might make in kindergarten—a rough, faded-red strawberry, badly sewn, with the stuffing coming out in one place, and a few pins stuck into it indicating its use.

Only the fourth object seemed worth saving. It was a square plaque of polished wood, on one face of which was carved a spray of flowers with tiny, drooping blossoms and sheathlike leaves. The work had been delicately, carefully carved, and Sandy replaced it with respect.

Except for the carving, these were puzzling items to be so treasured that they had been packed away in a box and hidden in this cabin drawer. Sandy was about to give up the mystery and put the cover back, when she noticed something flat lying on the bottom of the box. It proved to be two cut pieces of cardboard held together with a rubber band. Curiously, Sandy drew off the band and separated the two small squares of cardboard. Between them lay a glossy snapshot in black and white. She carried it to a window so she could see the picture more clearly, and found it was of a young man and a young woman. The man held a small child balanced on his shoulder—a child who was probably two or three years old. The man was tall and thin and rather good-looking, the girl very pretty.

Quite suddenly Sandy realized what she was looking at. The pretty girl was Trina's mother, the man her father. Della and Charlie. And the laughing, happy child on the man's shoulder was Trina when she had been hardly more than a baby.

Sandy felt an unexpected tightening of her throat because of this happy scene that had been lost so long ago in the past. Once Trina must have had a loving family. Before her father had found family life too much for him and had gone away. Before her mother had died. She knew what the things in the box were. The perfume bottle must have belonged to Trina's mother, the rusty penknife to her father. And perhaps the rough little strawberry was something Trina herself had made long ago when she was small. Who had made the flower carving she could not tell.

Quickly Sandy slipped the snapshot between its protecting cardboard squares and tucked the packet into the box. She had no right to be looking at these private belongings of Trina's. Perhaps Trina no longer had any right to keep this box here in the cabin, but Sandy knew it must be replaced at once and that Trina must not know she had looked into it.

She covered the box and carried it to the open drawer below the bunk. But she was already too late. She knew it the moment she heard the door behind her open. Knew it before she heard Trina's outraged voice.

"What are you doing with my things?"

Sandy turned slowly, the shoe box still in her hands. She felt more helpless and dismayed than ever before in her life.

"I—I'm sorry—" she began.

Moving awkwardly, Trina crossed the room and snatched the box from Sandy, holding it in her arms as though it were a child she protected.

"What do you have to be so snoopy for? Why'd you come in here anyway?"

No matter how saddened Sandy might feel about the contents of the box, this was going too far.

"The cabin belongs to us now," she said quietly. "I didn't know you'd kept your things here."

"You looked inside the box, didn't you?" Trina demanded. "You snooped into my things!"

She looked so angry, with her dead-leaf-colored hair wind-tossed from outdoors and her green eyes snapping, that Sandy felt alarmed. Trina was a big girl for her age, and she looked strong and a bit threatening. Sandy would have liked to say that she had not looked into the box, but somehow this was too important a thing to deceive Trina about.

"I looked inside because I didn't know it was yours. There's no harm done. If you want to keep your box here, I won't touch it again."

Sandy realized now why the box was here. At home Trina's grandmother might have called these things trash and thrown them out.

But Trina gave her no thanks for the offer. "Of course, I'll keep it here! And you'd better stay out of this cabin. Mr. Seale said I could come here whenever I wanted. He said it could be just like mine."

Sandy tried to answer reasonably, even though she had begun to shake a little in the face of Trina's upsetting attack. "Mr. Seale is gone. He isn't coming back anymore. But you can still come to the cabin whenever you like. My father won't mind."

"Who cares if he minds!" Trina thrust the box into the drawer, slammed it shut, and stood up to face Sandy. "If you ever touch that box again—" slowly she began to advance upon Sandy and there was a real threat in her eyes.

Sandy made no further effort to reason. Trina was between her and the door and the way she looked was frightening. In desperation, Sandy used an old ruse that

she had read in a book. She tore her gaze away from
Trina and stared toward a window.

"Look at that!" she cried, and the fright in her voice
sounded real—because it was real.

Trina had not read many books and she did the natural
thing. She turned her head and looked toward the window.
In that instant Sandy darted past her and escaped through
the open door. Once outside, she ran as she had never run
before. She could hear Trina lumbering along behind her,
but for all that she was used to the woods, the other girl
did not handle her feet well, and she could not move as
fast as Sandy.

A second trail opened off the one she knew, and for
safety's sake Sandy took it. The cabin was out of sight
now, and probably Trina would follow the main path in
pursuing her. When she no longer heard the sounds of
someone following, Sandy stopped, thoroughly out of
breath, and leaned panting against a tree. Her change of
paths had been successful and Trina had gone off down
the other trail. The only trouble was that she now followed
the path that lay between Sandy and home. It was to be
hoped that she would think Sandy had reached the house
and would give up and go back to her grandfather's.

When she had caught her breath, Sandy began to re-
trace her steps, crunching over dead leaves, watching out
for roots that might trip her. For a while she walked between crowding trees, looking for the path from the cabin.
It seemed as though it should have come up by this time,
but of course she had been running before, while now she
was walking more slowly.

Nothing along the way looked either familiar or unfamiliar. All trees seemed alike to her. Unless there was a
cabin, or a chunk of rock to make the scene different, how
could she tell where she was? She did have a sense that the
woods were growing thicker, the trees pressing closer together, so that the way seemed to darken and become less
clear as she advanced.

The other path should certainly have come up by this
time. With a suddenness that made her catch her breath,
she realized that she was lost. She had simply walked out
into these hundred acres of woods that covered the mountain on their own land—to say nothing of adjacent
forests—with no thought of which turn she was taking or
how to get back. There were probably all sorts of trails

and turnoffs, and while she was running down that second path, she had stopped keeping track of where she went.

Anxiously she gazed up between the treetops, but there was no longer any sun to be seen up there. Patches of sky that showed between the trees were gray. The afternoon was growing late, and darkness came early on these December days. Already it seemed to be dusky under the trees. True, she still followed a rough trail—though it had not been as thoroughly cleared as the one she knew—and a trail must lead somewhere.

She began to walk faster, and soon made a disturbing discovery. A trail might very well lead only to other trails, so that she could keep going in a circle without ever breaking out of these forest depths. Several times she came to a Y where a choice of directions opened up—but she had not the faintest idea of which branching path to take. She began to call out for help, shouting until the nearby woods rang with the sound of her voice. There was no answer. While her voice sounded noisy enough close by, it vanished into a blotting paper of surrounding forest, so that it could not be heard beyond.

If only she knew in which direction the cabin lay. If necessary, she could spend the night in the cabin. But of course if she could find the cabin, she could also find her way home. Now all her earlier fear of the woods came surging back, stirring along her nerves, running a cold finger down her spine. It was utterly lonely here on the mountain. And there were wild animals. Perhaps animals that came out only at night. Bobcats and—and bears.

When she came to a log that had fallen across the path, she was so tired that she sat down on the rough bark, feeling tiny and unprotected with tall dark trees all around her, and the light fading from the sky. Wind was blowing harder now, and the thrashing sounds that went on overhead added to her sense of fear. The wind came rushing up the mountain with a great roaring—like the voice of a river that had broken its bounds and was flooding over the land. The air had grown much colder, and there was a damp smell on the wind. She remembered her father saying back in the city that the air sometimes felt like snow. There was that sort of feeling now. Snow! And she was lost in the woods.

When would they begin to worry about her? How

would they know where to look? How could they find her in the dark?

Think, she told herself. Think about all the books you've read. What do people do when they're lost in the woods?

A few ideas came to her. For one thing, she mustn't run wildly off in all directions. She must start marking the paths she walked along so she could tell which ones she had gone down before. And she must watch for landmarks. Not all of the forest looked alike, she could see, once she had opened her eyes and began to take notice. There were rocks, broken trees, clumps of evergreen among the bare brown branches. There were hundreds of markings, if only she had paid attention.

This log, for instance. It had fallen straight across the path, and she knew she had not climbed over it before. Now she must choose whether to go back along the way she had come to reach this point, or climb over the dead tree and continue in a new direction. And there was another thing that might help her. This particular section of the mountain had been cut through by the highway. So if she walked downhill, she would either find the main road, find her own house, or reach the valley, where there would surely be farms and homes. The only trouble was that she didn't know which way was down. The top of the mountain was broad and rolled gently up and down. As far as she could see through the trees, no way led precipitately down. No distant views were visible. Yet there had to be an end to the top of the mountain. If she could manage to walk long enough in one direction, the hill would eventually go down. But none of the paths she had followed so far were straight. They went curling around and crossing one another. To go straight meant cutting off through thick woods, leaving the trails behind, and she knew she could not do that. She did not dare.

Something light and cool touched her hand. A snowflake. She looked up anxiously and saw a swirling whiteness overhead. In moments the snow began to fall. And she was wearing only jeans and a sweater. Huddling upon the log, she fought back frightened tears. All this was Trina's fault. If she hadn't been so mean and threatening, Sandy would never have run off and gotten lost in the woods. When she was back home again, she meant to tell everyone exactly how awful Trina had been.

But right now what was happening didn't seem entirely real. How could a girl from New York City find herself lost so completely upon a New Jersey mountainside? It was like a dream, a nightmare. But it was neither. It was real enough. And this was no time to sit here and cry.

Girls in books took action. They didn't sit down and weep over their predicaments. Taking action seemed a good plan for real life too. Sandy stood up on the fallen tree and looked around. The snow was drifting down quite thickly now, and beginning to coat branches with a lining of white. Already it had begun to carpet the trail along which she had come. And her jeans and sweater were covered with wet white fluff.

She beat the snow from her clothes with hands that were a little frantic. Then she climbed over the log and went on along the fresh trail. Going back through the maze that had already confused her wouldn't do any good. For all she knew, this way might be shorter. And at least the fallen tree was a landmark. From now on she would watch for every branching of the path, and she would find a way to mark the path along which she had come. She could use stones and broken twigs for that. At least she would mark it as long as she could see. It was definitely growing darker now. But the swirling whiteness held the light, and she could still see her way.

Having a plan and doing something about it helped. But she was still frightened, and every minute she grew colder. She began to run to keep herself warm, and when she stopped, she jumped up and down and flapped her arms. Once, startling her, a deer walked out of the swirling snow and stood looking at her with calm interest. But it was a wild thing, and it was too close. Sandy stood very still, and after a moment the deer dismissed her as a creature of no importance, and walked quietly away among the trees.

When the first sound of voices reached her, she could hardly believe in them. The sound was probably only the wind and the swishing snow. But the wind would not be calling her name. There—it came again: "Sandy! Sandy!"

She cupped her hands about her mouth and shouted in reply. "Here I am! Right over here! Here I am!" She turned in different directions, shouting, and answering calls came back to her. Now she could hear a trampling along the path, and in a moment Trina Carpozi came out of the woods around a turn.

Even Trina was a welcome sight, but she was not alone. Cliff Wendel was close behind, and he carried Sandy's winter coat over one arm. He helped her into it and made no remarks about how dumb she was to get lost in the woods. Trina took care of that.

"How stupid can you get!" she demanded. "If it wasn't for me, you'd have to stay in the woods all night. Don't you have any more sense than to go wandering around on the mountain when you don't know your way?"

"Oh, lay off!" Cliff said. "You could get lost in a city just as easily, Trina. Let's get Sandy back to her house."

Trina did not seem to mind Cliff's words, but Sandy had no heart for arguing with her. She couldn't even feel indignant, but only grateful because these two had come looking for her.

"How did you find me?" she asked Cliff, as they fell in behind Trina on the winding trail, following her as she clumped along, her right foot moving awkwardly.

"Your dad went up in the woods as far as the cabin and back," Cliff said. "Then he phoned my father. I came over to see if I could help, and when it began to get dark, I got Trina. She's the one who knows every inch of the trails through these woods. So your father took one direction, and Trina and I took another."

"But even then—" Sandy said, "I don't see how—"

Trina heard her and tossed words over her shoulder. "We only had to start at the place where you went off the main path when you were running away from me. I know all the turns, and if we followed them, we'd have to find you. There're miles of trails up here, but they're not endless. We were lucky to find you so quickly."

Cliff caught up her words. "Why was she running away from you, Trina?"

Trina tossed her head. She hadn't bothered to put on a cap and snowflakes frosted her winter-leaf hair. "You'd better ask *her*."

Cliff looked at Sandy, but she walked quickly ahead of him without answering. Somehow she no longer wanted to tell anyone about Trina's box, and how she had behaved in the cabin—how all this had been her fault. When she said nothing, Trina turned her head again to glance at her, and there was a faint look of surprise on her usually sullen face. As if she had expected angry blame.

After that they did not talk, but ducked their heads

against the blowing snow, hurrying along breathlessly as they followed Trina's lead. Now and then they stopped to make Indian calls, clapping their hands over their mouths, to signal Sandy's father that she had been found. Eventually they heard an answer, and by the time they reached the main trail he was waiting for them. He hugged Sandy in relief, and for the moment asked no questions.

By the time they reached the house, the snow had stopped, proving itself to have been only a thick flurry. But the trees had been frosted with the first white of winter, the green grass around the house was coated with white, and the roof wore a layer of cotton. Nothing could have looked more wonderful to Sandy than the lighted windows of her new home, or the fire that roared in the living room grate. Mother ushered them in before the fire at once, and enveloped Sandy in a loving hug that told her daughter what a fright her mother had had. Dad scolded a little, but was mainly interested in thanking Cliff.

"It was Trina who found her," Cliff said.

They all looked around for Trina, but the girl was gone. No one was sure—in the excitement over greeting Sandy—whether she had even come into the house. She had simply disappeared. In spite of everything, Sandy felt a little sorry. Prickly though Trina was, Sandy wished she could have been thanked and praised. Sandy had a feeling that praise probably didn't come Trina's way very often. Anyway—there was tomorrow. Tomorrow she would thank her. And Cliff would tell his father what Trina had done, so perhaps Mr. Wendel would let his class know about it.

After Cliff had gone, the thought continued to be vaguely comforting in spite of the contradictory feeling Sandy had about Trina. She wasn't an especially likable girl, yet those small hidden objects in the shoe box up in the cabin had given Sandy an aching sort of feeling. On the other hand, Trina had ordered her out of the cabin which belonged to Sandy's father, and she'd been entirely unpleasant, even mean. Probably she had only come hunting through the woods because Cliff had made her do it.

Sandy warmed her chilled hands at the fire and thought about her mixed-up emotions.

"You're quiet," Mother said. "There's something deep going on, isn't there?"

Sandy looked at her doubtfully. She just couldn't talk

about all this. Not yet. First she had to figure out a few things for herself and find out where she really stood. Only a little while ago she had been so sure that Trina was none of her business. Trina could be ignored. Now she was no longer positive that this was so. The pattern had changed in some way, so that whether she or Trina liked it or not, the threads of their lives had been tangled together, and it was going to be hard to be free of each other. One of them might have to cut that thread quite roughly to be free. And probably Trina was the one who would do it. She had begun tonight by just walking away from the house instead of coming inside to be thanked.

Perhaps Sandy should feel glad of that. She certainly didn't want to feel indebted to someone she did not like.

Mother reminded her that they were to go to the Wendels' for supper, and Sandy stopped thinking about Trina as she went to change her clothes and get ready.

5

Invisible Girl

The first day of school!

Sandy wakened early with a sense of anticipation that was not wholly pleasant. Even though she knew a few of the girls and had met Mr. Wendel, a certain uneasiness remained. Things that weren't known were always a little scary, though often when you learned about them, you found there hadn't been all that much to worry about. She must remember that. Still—she wasn't sure.

Mother offered to drive her out to the road and wait until she boarded the school bus, but Dad said that was nonsense. Country kids learned to walk. It was a privilege they had that city children had lost. In fact, in his day he'd have had to walk the whole way in to the village.

Dad was right, of course—though for a different reason than his daughter's—and Sandy said she would walk to the highway. Only small children were put on the buses by their mothers. She could imagine how Trina—and perhaps even Melissa—would laugh if she was taken to the bus. So when the time came she started down the road alone.

There was no one in sight around the Wendel house. When they had gone to supper there last night Mr. Wendel had said that he usually drove in early and that Cliff rode his bike to school unless the weather was too bad. Since the dusting of snow was already melting from the road surface in the warm morning sunshine, Cliff would have gone by now.

Sandy had started in plenty of time, so she did not have to hurry. She ambled along the curving road with eyes that were newly alert to everything around her. Since yesterday's experience in the woods, she meant to look at her surroundings more closely and keep track of where she was. Perhaps she didn't exactly like the country, but she had learned to respect it.

In fact, Mr. Wendel had talked about this very thing at supper last night—about being aware of one's surroundings. He had a project he meant to propose to his class on Monday, and he wondered if Dad would mind if, at various times, groups of children came up to visit the woods and the new pond which Mr. Seale had built last summer. There was a great deal to be learned at firsthand up there. Of course Dad said that would be fine, and Sandy was pleased. She could imagine herself leading the way through woods she would by then know better than anyone else. If Trina could learn those paths, so could she.

As she neared the highway, she heard footsteps on the road behind her, and she turned to see Trina following. There was nothing to do but stop and wait for the other girl to catch up. But when Sandy stopped on the road Trina stopped too, staring at her blankly. After an uncomfortable moment of this, Sandy went on toward the highway. The thought was still in her mind that she ought to thank Trina for what she had done yesterday, but plainly this was not going to be invited. Anyway, Trina's behavior made ignoring her that much easier, and Sandy went toward the bus stop with a feeling that a load she did not want to carry had been slightly eased for her. If Trina wanted to avoid her, that made everything much simpler.

The bus stop was across the road and two or three mothers were there with small children. Sandy was able to stand on one side of the little group, while Trina stayed on the other. When the yellow school bus pulled to a stop with its lights blinking, Sandy got on first, with Trina right behind her. Halfway down the aisle, Melissa, who had boarded at an earlier stop, was sitting with an empty place next to her. She saw Sandy coming and waved to her cheerfully.

"Come and sit by me!"

Sandy dropped into the seat, pleased to be asked, and Melissa laughed.

"Saved you, didn't I?"

"Saved me?" Sandy repeated.

"From having to sit with that awful Trina," Melissa said.

Sandy was uncomfortably aware of Melissa's loud voice and of the fact that Trina's place was one seat back across the aisle. Trina could never have missed hearing Melissa's words. Some of the children nearby heard and looked around.

"Ssh!" Sandy said. "She can hear you."

"Of course. I meant her to. Don't look back. We'll pretend she's invisible. That's it—that's what we'll do today! We'll all pretend we can't see her at all. Trina's our project this term, you know. We've been thinking up different things to do about her. We take turns, so if you come in with us, you'll get a turn too. You'd better start thinking up something good."

Sandy cast a quick look at the girl beside her. Melissa was gazing out of the window, smiling happily. She looked like such an attractive girl, and she was obviously popular and had a great many friends. Things would be much easier for Sandy in school if Melissa was on her side. But she shrank from the thing Melissa was proposing. She couldn't imagine other girls following such a lead.

"Yesterday I got lost in the woods," she told Melissa. "I mean really lost. They had to send for Trina to come and find me. She and Cliff came up through some of those trails and located me. Otherwise I might have had to spend the night in the woods."

Melissa seemed unimpressed. "Sure. That's like putting a dog on your trail. Trina's half wild. Why shouldn't she find you?"

Sandy was glad of the rattling of the bus and the chatter of the other children. This time Melissa's words would not have been overheard. But all the rest of the way into the village, Sandy felt an almost irresistible urge to turn her head and look at Trina. She managed not to because she could imagine the blank stare she would get in return. Trina probably wouldn't even care if the others pretended she was invisible.

The Halcyon school was built on a hillside on the far side of town. The bus ran over a stone bridge and through the tiny business section before it turned up a blacktop drive into the parking place at the side of the old redbrick building that had a new annex built on as a wing. The moment the bus stopped, the children poured out into the school yard. Melissa held Sandy back until Trina got into the aisle just ahead of them. Then she pushed Sandy along.

"Hurry up," she said. "There's nobody ahead of you. What are you poking along for?"

Sandy, who was practically stepping on Trina's heels, stopped dead still in the aisle and waited until Trina got

off the bus. The children behind Melissa had begun to
shove and push, and Melissa was not pleased.

"What did you do that for?" she asked as they went
down the bus steps. "Aren't you going to play our game?"

"I don't think so," Sandy said, and walked away by herself. For the moment she did not want to be near either
Trina or Melissa. She did not like either of them, and she
was beginning to feel sure she wasn't going to like this
new school either. She had a sudden deep yearning for the
school she knew back in New York. There had been problems there too. There were always problems. But she had
been able to handle them. Now it seemed as though something was happening, through no fault of hers, that was
too big for her to handle. She wished Cliff were younger,
so he might be in the same homeroom. Cliff was the sort
of person who would know how to meet difficult problems
and do the right thing. But he had his own, older friends,
and she would probably see little of him in school.

This morning there was the business of checking into
the office to register as a new pupil, and she did not reach
her room until the other boys and girls were already at
work. Mrs. Venner, the school principal, took Sandy to
Mr. Wendel's room and left her there. He looked up from
his desk and gave her a welcoming smile, his eyes friendly
behind the thick lenses of his glasses. Sandy sensed at once
that he was a different person in a schoolroom. This was
where he wanted to be, and she had a feeling that teaching
was what he liked best to do. Behind his desk, set in one
corner of the room near a window, he no longer looked
slight and unimpressive.

"This is Sandra—Sandy Forster, from New York," Mr.
Wendel told the class. "Sandy, since you already know
Melissa Morris, I'm going to give you the seat next to her.
Melissa, will you show Sandy where to hang her things?"

Melissa obviously took no pleasure in this assigned task.
At one side of the room two stationary dividers that held
bright orange tack boards hid the coatracks. Green, red,
and yellow hooks were already loaded with coats, but Melissa found her an empty one and Sandy took off her
things, aware of curious looks from the rest of the room.
Then, still reluctant, Melissa led her to the empty desk
next to her own.

Gray desks and green chairs were arranged in a deep
U-shape around the room, and there was a long table

across the open end of the U, where Mr. Wendel could stand and talk, with various books and visual aids before him. While he was their homeroom teacher, he also taught earth sciences.

As Sandy sat down, he spoke to her again. "We're having a reading period right now, Sandy. There's a book on your desk, and you can turn to page twelve. That's the introductory chapter on ecology. We're going to discuss it in a little while."

From across the room Debra Elliot gave her a smile of welcome, and Sandy was grateful for that, at least. She was uncomfortably aware that Trina sat on her right, two desks away, glowering at the book before her.

The classroom was one of the most cheerful she had ever seen. Though the building was old, this room was in the new section, and everything looked fresh and bright. Sun poured in along one side, and there were plants on a table near the windows. Books with bright jackets, and magazines opened to show illustrations, were spread along a table. A round blue globe of the world stood on a corner shelf. At one end of a blackboard was a bulletin board with newspaper clippings and pictures and notes tacked to it, art posters painted by the children were displayed on the orange dividers. On Mr. Wendel's corner desk stood a green vase filled with decorative branches to which bright autumn leaves still clung. It was an interesting, colorful room, and Sandy began to relax a little at her desk. She turned to page twelve and started to read.

The chapter on ecology had to do with various phases of saving the environment. Sandy had already studied quite a bit about air and water pollution in her New York school, so she did not feel this was a subject unknown to her. Nevertheless, when the discussion period came, she did not put up her hand to offer anything. She had talked easily enough in the school she was used to, but now she felt shy and self-conscious, all too much aware of the strange eyes fixed upon her. Mr. Wendel seemed to understand this, and he let a number of children talk before he called on her. Then he got her to talk a little about problems faced by cities as opposed to the country problems with which Halcyon was familiar.

Both boys and girls in the room stared at her curiously while she talked, measuring her as a new girl, and she found she could not think very clearly under their eyes, so that her words came haltingly. Mr. Wendel helped by asking questions she could answer easily, and in the end she felt she had not disgraced herself. From two seats away she heard a disparaging grunt, and knew that it came from Trina. There was nothing she could do of which Trina would approve. Especially not since that bus ride this morning.

"Speaking of our environment," Mr. Wendel went on, "I'm afraid very few of us, even those living in the country, with woods and farmlands and lakes easily accessible, know as much about these things as we should. This term I hope we can take a few trips and initiate a few projects that will help correct this lack. Last year, you remember, Mr. Seale came to visit the school and spoke to us in assembly. He told us a great deal about wildlife and its preservation. This year perhaps some of us can go up to what is now Mr. Forster's woods and find out a bit more at firsthand. Sandy Forster had an experience up there yesterday, when she got lost on the trails. That was natural enough and could happen to any of us. Fortunately, Trina Carpozi, who knows more about those woods than anyone else, was able to find her, and she and my son, Cliff, brought Sandy home. That was a good job, Trina."

Nearly everyone turned to stare at Trina, who in turn continued to stare at her book. Only Melissa looked straight ahead and did not move her eyes in Trina's direction.

Mr. Wendel did not dwell on the rescue, but went quickly on to other matters, though he still spoke about Trina.

"One of the exciting things that Mr. Seale did on his property last summer was to build a large pond. Trina had a good opportunity to watch it being built, and I hope she'll share her knowledge with us when we go up to see it. Does anyone know why the building of ponds is encouraged by the U.S. Conservation Service?"

No one raised a hand, but Trina squirmed a little in her seat.

"I think you can tell us, Trina," Mr. Wendel said.

She turned her glowering look upon him and blurted out a few words. "Sure! It helps to raise the water table and preserve water." Her scorn was even more evident as she spoke, as though she thought everyone ought to know this.

Mr. Wendel nodded pleasantly. He was trying hard, Sandy knew, to draw Trina out and get her to take part in the discussion. Most everyone wanted to contribute something that the others would respect and approve of, and this was Trina's chance to take an active role in what was happening. But drawing Trina out was like trying to coax a turtle from its shell. The more you coaxed, the deeper in the turtle drew its head.

"What happens if there are no ponds?" Mr. Wendel asked. But this time Trina would not answer.

"Suppose we try to find that out," Mr. Wendel said to the room. "And now I'd like to set up several groups—committees—that will study various phases of our environment. We can study the town, some nearby farms, the stream that runs through Halcyon, Mr. Seale's—that is, Mr. Forster's—woods and pond, and so on. I'll look for some good reports from these committee members."

He began calling out names and writing them down on a slip of paper. To her dismay, Sandy found that she, Trina, Melissa, Ginger, and Debra had been placed together as one group. That was awful. Didn't Mr. Wendel realize that Melissa was the leader when it came to teasing Trina? But there was nothing she could say or do to stop what was happening.

When the bell rang for recess, she was glad to get up from her desk and file outside with the others. The sixth and seventh grades had recess at the same time, with Mr. Wendel in charge of the boys, and the seventh-grade woman teacher in charge of the girls. Apparently this was a time for organized play, but instead of joining in Melissa slyly drew to one side, with several girls around her—among them Debra and Ginger. Obviously, she was a leader in the class with many of the girls, and it was becoming increasingly clear that unless Sandy made friends with her, she would be left out of what happened at school.

Trina ambled off by herself, watching some girls skipping rope but not joining in. Sandy ducked out of the way of several boys who were playing ball, and walked around idly until Melissa suddenly waved to her. Glad of someone to join, Sandy went over to Melissa's group.

"Mom said I was to be nice to you," Melissa told her sweetly, "so if you want to come along with us, you can." She was bouncing a basketball, probably to give the impression of play, and she kept a wary eye on the supervising teacher.

This was a left-handed way in which to be invited to join Melissa's group, Sandy thought, but at the moment she had no other choice—unless she wanted to stand apart like Trina, or try to make friends with others in the class who were still strangers and paying no attention to her in the midst of their games.

Melissa and her friends had been whispering and now they grouped close together and started across the playground, Sandy moving uneasily with them and Melissa still bouncing her ball.

"I don't see how we can pretend she's invisible," Debra whispered. "That's hard to do."

"Of course we can!" Melissa was assured as always. "Look—it's that spot on the ground," she said as they drew near Trina. "It looks like tar, doesn't it? We'll have to be careful or we'll get it on our shoes."

She was bouncing the ball—bouncing it almost at Trina's feet. Trina backed away and Melissa followed. Sandy hung back unhappily. The other girls were suppressing a tendency to giggle and their eyes danced as they circled around Trina.

"We'll have to jump over that tarry spot, won't we?" Melissa said. "You go first, Debra."

Debra tossed her ponytails and walked directly toward Trina. In spite of herself, Trina fell back two more steps before this determined advance, and Debra made a big thing out of jumping over the spot where Trina had stood.

"There was something in the air over there," Debra told the others, choking back her laughter. "I can't see anything, but it feels as though there's something there."

Ginger tried it next, and she bumped right into Trina, who again fell back because she didn't understand what they were doing. When Ginger had jumped, Melissa waved to Sandy. "It's your turn. Go ahead."

"I don't want to," Sandy said.

Melissa's smile never lost its sweetness. "You'd better, you know. Otherwise you might become invisible too. Isn't that so, girls?"

There was more nodding and laughing, but Debra came over to Sandy and spoke in a kindly enough way.

"Go ahead, Sandy. This is fun, and Trina's too dumb to know what it's all about."

A choice had to be made. Why should she sacrifice the chance to become one of Melissa's friends simply for the sake of Trina, who wouldn't thank her in any case? She drew a deep breath and walked directly toward Trina. This time, however, Trina did not mean to take any more. She stood her ground and scowled at Sandy, her fists doubled and ready to fly. She looked as threatening as she had in the cabin yesterday, but at least there were others around, and Sandy was less afraid.

She took several more steps in Trina's direction, while the others watched. She was really on the spot, and she knew it. If she got close enough, Trina would hit her. If she backed away, Melissa's crowd would laugh, and she would be through as far as they were concerned.

Sandy acted with a sudden burst of speed, darting in close to Trina so that she was taken by surprise, ducking in under her raised fists, and then dashing away. Yesterday she had seen how clumsily Trina moved, and she was sure she could move faster. Pleased with her effort, she ran a few steps farther and bumped right into Cliff Wendel. He had been watching, and when she'd righted herself, he gave her a look of disgust and walked away.

Melissa called, "That was good, Sandy!"

It was time to go in, and Sandy had an excuse to turn her back on the other girls and walk toward the school building. She no longer felt pleased. Cliff's look had told her what she had done, and she felt thoroughly miserable. Maybe Trina was impossible, maybe she deserved the treatment she got, but, at the same time, everyone had feelings, and what Melissa's group had done had been cruel. Trina must have minded, even if she told herself she didn't. Anyone would mind.

She could take little comfort in the fact that Debra came to walk in the building with her and talked to her in a friendly way that meant acceptance. She liked Debra and she would like her friendship. But she hated to think of the price she had paid for it.

The rest of the day seemed to creep by. Even when they changed rooms for other classes and she met new teachers, the cloud of self-reproach hung over her, so that she couldn't find her usual interest in new experiences.

When school was dismissed at two thirty, Debra came with Sandy when she walked out of the room, and the two went with Melissa and Ginger to the bus. Everyone was carrying books, and Sandy had some to carry this time. Melissa had been whispering again, but now she included Sandy.

"Ginger's thought up a wonderful idea for tomorrow," Melissa said. "I'll tell you about it on the bus, Sandy. We can start on the way to school in the morning. So long for now, Ginger. Debra, will you come over to my house soon—if your mother can bring you? It's your turn to come to see me."

"What about that ecology project?" Ginger said. "How can we ever work with Trina?"

"We won't. We'll just pretend she isn't there—the way we did today. Or we can use tomorrow's plan. That may be even better."

Sandy found herself boarding the bus to sit beside Melissa at the back. This time Trina sat in front and never once turned her head in their direction. She was trying to stay away from her tormentors, but Sandy had a sinking feeling that it would do no good.

On the way home, Melissa explained the new plan.

"Tomorrow we'll pretend that Trina has a contagious disease. Whenever we get near her, we'll scream and jump away. If we touch her, we'll dust ourselves off as if we were afraid of catching whatever it is. Maybe I can fix up a sign that says SMALLPOX and we can find a way to pin it on Trina's back."

Sandy did not enjoy the bus ride home. Her stomach seemed to be churning, and she felt a deepening dislike for Halcyon, the school, the mountain, Melissa and her friends—everything. And especially for Sandy Forster. She was overcome by a longing to be back in New York where her real friends were, and where she knew her way around and would never get lost. Where no one expected her to play mean tricks in order to earn friendship.

Melissa talked to her on the way home, but Sandy hardly heard her words and she made no response to them. Since Melissa enjoyed talking, she did not seem to notice Sandy's silence. When the bus stopped for their road, Trina got off first and went ahead. Sandy left the bus well behind her and followed more slowly. She had an uneasy feeling that Trina might turn on her resentfully here on this lonely road, but the other girl marched straight ahead with her lopsided gait, and never looked around.

Before Sandy reached the Wendel house, Cliff came along on his bicycle and stopped beside her. She gave him a quick, guilty glance and then looked away. But he seemed to have forgotten the distaste he'd shown for her on the playground. He got off his bike and pushed it along beside her.

"How did you like our school?" Cliff asked.

"It was okay," Sandy said carefully. Cliff was the one person to whom she didn't dare betray her feelings. He might not sympathize with her longing to have friends and be popular in school.

"It takes a little while," Cliff said.

She doubted if that had been true for him. He was the sort of person who would probably fit in anywhere easily. He didn't look as though he would be troubled by a lot of mixed-up feelings and wishes that contradicted each other. At least there was one question she could ask him because he was close to Mr. Wendel.

She explained about the ecology project his father had proposed, and told how he had broken the room up into various "committees." Some were of boys alone, some were boys and girls mixed, and some were just girls' groups.

"Why didn't he have us all boys and girls?" she asked, starting out cautiously.

Cliff grinned. "Just testing, I guess. Dad talked about that at home the other day. He wants to see what differences come out of these combinations—whether they'll all do the same things and come up with the same results, whether they'll work the same way, or whether the different combinations will have different approaches."

"That sounds all right," Sandy said. "But why did he put Trina with Melissa and Debra and Ginger? Doesn't he know those girls are teasing Trina?" She found herself speaking hesitantly, because she had been teasing her too, and Cliff knew it. But he made no point of that.

"I'm not sure. I know he'd like to help Trina. You notice he put you in that group too."

"How did you know?"

"He said he would," Cliff told her. "After all, Trina rescued you yesterday, so that should make you feel friendly toward her."

"Maybe it should, but it didn't. She doesn't want any friends!"

"Do you believe that?"

"I don't know what I believe." She was beginning to feel a little desperate and she didn't want to be cornered. "I only know those girls will pick on Trina, and she'll fight them—and the whole project will be spoiled. It could be interesting too. Why didn't he put Trina somewhere else?"

"Do you think she'd fit in better anywhere else?"

"How do I know?" Sandy had a feeling that both Cliff and his father were putting pressure on her to help Trina—and stand against the other girls. But she didn't want to do that. What she really wanted was to be friends with everyone, and that didn't seem possible.

Cliff speculated out loud, paying no attention to her grumpy tone. "Trina isn't stupid, you know. Dad says she's got a good I.Q. But she's slow in school because she's not interested in anything. She's had a lot of trouble, and things aren't right for her at home with her grandmother. At school they're worse. One way she's not like the other kids is that she has a foot that should have been taken care of when she was small, and wasn't. So now she needs an operation. This makes her seem awkward and slow. She feels all this, and knows she's different, so she's begun to slap out at everybody. I expect Dad put her with this group hoping she might prove to these girls how much she really knows about outdoor things. Perhaps they'll begin to respect her even if they don't like her. Maybe if she could find her own place, she'd stop fighting everybody."

"But she's not like anybody else," Sandy objected. "She looks funny. Her hair is messy all the time, and she doesn't care how she dresses."

"Dad says those things might change if she started to be interested in school. Anyway, she *is* different. She's not a rubber stamp of everybody else. Neither were a lot of people who grew up to be famous and successful just being themselves. Who knows what Trina might become?"

Sandy had to laugh at that. She couldn't imagine Trina becoming anything of consequence unless she changed her ways.

"Being different makes it hard for her," Cliff went on. "You know what happens with animals when a *different* one is born in a litter?"

Sandy shook her head.

"Sometimes the other animals kill it. Or they push it out

to live or die by itself. Isn't that what Melissa is trying to do to Trina? Push her out?"

That was a dreadful thought. Sandy hated the picture of a small, helpless animal being driven away by its fellows. Nevertheless, she could not fit Trina into that picture. Trina might stand alone, but she was anything but helpless.

"I don't like Melissa any better than I do Trina," Sandy admitted.

"Neither do I," Cliff said. "But Melissa's changed a lot since her father died. I guess she misses him."

Sandy couldn't see what that had to do with anything, but she let it go. This talk wasn't helping her to solve an impossible problem.

They'd reached Cliff's house, but he did not turn in the driveway at once.

"Would you like to go down to the Haineses and see Sam's workshop?" he asked.

Sandy did not want to especially, since Trina was likely to be there. But so far Cliff was the only person she could regard as a friend, so she nodded. At least it would be something to do.

"I'll go put my books away," she said.

"Okay. I'll meet you at the foot of your drive in about twenty minutes."

Sandy hurried home to have a quick glass of milk and a peanut butter sandwich in the kitchen, while Mother asked her about school. Sandy told her about Mr. Wendel and his classroom, and Mother listened with interest, quite taken by the ecology project.

"We can all learn something useful there," she said. "I know very little about this country environment. So I can learn from you while you're learning. And what a good thing that Trina Carpozi is to be in your group. She can teach all of you about these woods."

Sandy said nothing. She had a feeling that Trina would teach them nothing if she could help it.

6

Incident at the Bus

Sam Haines had built his workshop in one half of a two-car garage. He had put in a space heater so he could work there in winter, and to Sandy's eyes his workbench and shelves and tools were the most orderly she'd ever seen.

Today Mr. Haines wore overalls and a shapeless gray sweater, and there were various chisels and other tools sticking out of his hip pockets. He seemed accustomed to having Cliff visit him here and he greeted them both with a welcoming grin.

"Going to finish up that tray you're working on for Christmas, Cliff?" he asked as they came into the tidy shop.

"Maybe I'll do some work on it," Cliff said. "Anyway, I'd like to show it to Sandy."

From a shelf he brought down a handsome wooden tray, explaining that it was a gift for his mother, and that he had finished it except for sanding and varnishing.

When Sandy had admired it, Cliff set it on Mr. Haines's long workbench and went to work on it with sandpaper.

"Are you interested in woodworking?" Mr. Haines asked Sandy.

"I've never thought much about it," Sandy said.

"Trina doesn't care for it," Mr. Haines went on. "But you take her mother now—Della was a girl who could make nice things out of wood. She always liked to come out and work in my shop. Look at this."

He reached up on a shelf and brought down the carving of a small, prancing horse. It was a beautiful thing, and Sandy held it in her hands carefully. The mane seemed to blow in a wind, and the tail was arched and flowing, as if the animal were really alive. The wood had been lovingly polished to a glossy brown that seemed a natural color for the little horse.

As she stood with the carving in her hand, the door creaked open and she looked around to see Trina come into the shop. The other girl cast a quick glance of resentment at Sandy, and then went to sit on a high stool in one corner of the shop, where she stared stolidly around the room.

Her grandfather seemed used to her manner and paid no attention. "Now you take Trina," he said conversationally to Sandy, "she's not a bit interested in wood carving, but she sure knows about animals and growing things. My Della was the one who loved carving. Here's something else she made."

He replaced the horse and brought down another small figure from the shelf. This time it was a carving of a pioneer woman in a long dress and sunbonnet, holding a baby in her arms. Sandy took it from him, feeling uncomfortable under Trina's eyes, and turned it about in her hands.

The carver had given her greatest attention to the face, and Sandy had the feeling that this was a woman who was afraid. She seemed to look off into the distance as though she saw something terrible approaching—some dreadful thing she had to stand and face.

"She—she looks frightened," Sandy said, wondering if Della too had known what fear was like.

Mr. Haines nodded. "Indians, maybe? I asked her once, but she wouldn't ever say." He sighed. "Even now it's hard to believe that Della's gone and these little things she made are still here."

Trina wriggled on her stool. "I know what she was afraid of—that woman my mother carved."

Neither her grandfather nor Sandy said anything, but Cliff looked up from his tray. "Tell us, then."

Trina closed her eyes as though she watched an inner picture, and the hard, angry expression on her face softened.

"That woman's husband went off into the woods, and she was afraid he'd never come back. She was afraid she couldn't live where she was and take care of the baby all by herself."

Her grandfather nodded gently. "Maybe you've got something there. Anyway, she was good at this sort of thing—my Della. If she'd just gone ahead to school the way we wanted, she might have done something good with her carving. She might even be alive now."

"But I wouldn't be," Trina said bluntly.

"That's right, isn't it?" Her grandfather seemed to consider this. "And I guess I'm pretty glad you are here, so I shouldn't go thinking about what can't be changed."

Trina made a rough, snorting sound, as though she didn't believe anyone was glad to have her here. She hopped down from her stool, snatched the small figure of the pioneer woman from Sandy's hands and carried it back to the niche where her grandfather kept it. Mr. Haines watched her in a troubled way, but he did not chide her, and when Trina went out of the door and slammed it behind her, he shook his head sadly.

"It's hard to know what to do," he said, half to himself.

"Dad thinks Trina can help a lot with the ecology project he's started in school," Cliff said. "He's put her on a committee with Sandy and some other girls. They're going up to Sandy's woods and find out about trees and what they do for the environment and about that pond Mr. Seale put in up there."

"That's good," Mr. Haines said. "Trina knows about things like that. The only trouble is—will she help out?"

There seemed to be no answer to that. Mr. Haines brought Sandy a chunk of wood and a carving gouge. "You might as well be busy," he said. "Just play around with the wood, and get the feel of scooping into it. But watch your fingers."

He returned to his own work of mending a ladderback chair, while Cliff sanded. No one talked, and the silence was pleasant with everyone busy. A bit awkwardly Sandy gouged out slivers of wood with the scooped tool, but she was thinking of the carving that Della Carpozi had made of the pioneer woman with the frightened look on her face, and of what Trina had said about the carving—that it was of a woman who was afraid her husband would never come back to her. As Della herself had been afraid?

After a while, Cliff looked out of the shop window and broke the silence. "Look—it's snowing again. The weather report said we might get a good bit tonight."

Sandy stopped her work with the gouge and looked out the window, watching the snow as it floated gently down past the glass. Perhaps if it snowed hard enough, there wouldn't be any school tomorrow, and then she wouldn't have to watch what Melissa and her friends meant to do to Trina Carpozi. Or even if there was school, perhaps she would be able to stay home because it would be deep out here. And that would have the same result.

Cliff seemed to read her mind. "They always plow out the mountain road—the highway—and sand it, because there's a lot of traffic on it. And the county's pretty good about plowing our side road. So you won't have to worry about not getting to school tomorrow, unless it's very bad."

"I wasn't worrying," Sandy said. She had only been hoping.

By the time she left the shop with Cliff and started home, the world was beautifully white and the flakes were coming down thickly and steadily from the sky. There seemed to be no wind to turn the snowfall into a storm, and everything was hushed and quiet.

Cliff left Sandy at the foot of her drive and she started up the hill. Already the evergreens were frosted with white, but now there was no terror for her at the sight of snow, as there had been when she was lost in the woods. A squirrel went springing across the lawn toward his own winter shelter in an old tree, and she could see the tiny footprints he left in the fresh snow.

Somehow there was comfort in a world that looked as peaceful as this. All the ugliness that surrounded Trina seemed to fall away and leave Sandy free. She went into the house feeling more lighthearted than at any time today. She was happy to tell her mother about Sam Haines's workshop and of her experience in using a gouge on a piece of wood.

Cliff was right. There was school the next day. For one thing, the snow had ended during the night, and the Forsters rose to a glistening white day, with the sun shining on distant snowfields. All around the house the white blanket lay unmarked and clean—very different from grimy city snow that began to get dirty, even as it fell.

"Perhaps we'll have a white Christmas," Mother said, as she saw Sandy to the door.

Boots were in order this morning, and Sandy enjoyed stamping through the light drifts and looking at the white world around her as she walked. In front of Cliff's house she could see the tracks where he had rolled out his bicycle and walked beside it along the road. Apparently he had expected to be able to ride on the highway.

Trina was not in sight, and there were no other marks

besides those of Mr. Wendel's car and Cliff's bike tracks. Once Sandy looked back to examine her own prints in the snow, and saw Trina coming far behind. This time she knew better than to wait for her, and she hurried on to the bus stop.

To her surprise Melissa was there, looking pretty in blue ski pants, white boots on her feet, and a fuzzy white cap on her head. She waved at Sandy from across the road, and when Sandy crossed she came over to her at once, speaking in a low tone, so the mothers who waited with their younger charges would not hear.

"I walked down here instead of waiting for the bus at my house," Melissa said. "So now we can start in right away."

"Start in?" Sandy repeated, hating to have all the ugliness begin again.

Melissa nudged her. "Look—here comes Clumpy across the road. Watch what I'm going to do."

Helplessly, Sandy watched. Already her sense of peace because of the snow and the clean white world was fading. Why did it have to be *people* who spoiled the peace? Melissa stood near where Trina crossed the road, and when Trina would have gone past, paying no attention to her, Melissa leaped frantically out of her way and gave a little screech. Then she flew over to Sandy and snatched her out of Trina's path. "Look out—it's catching!" she cried.

The bus had arrived and mothers were busy getting their small children aboard, so they paid no attention to Melissa. Neither did Trina pay any attention as she walked toward the bus. Again Melissa dragged Sandy away from her.

"Don't touch her! Be careful! It's terribly catching!"

Sandy said, "Oh, don't be silly," and fell in behind Trina as she boarded the bus.

"Traitor!" Melissa whispered in her ear.

Feeling thoroughly unhappy, Sandy found a seat by herself and tried not to look at either Trina or Melissa the rest of the way.

When the bus reached the school yard, she got off quickly, ahead of the others, to disengage herself from what Melissa was doing. But she could not help seeing that Debra and Ginger rallied around Melissa, and all three were performing touch-me-not antics as they circled Trina. The worst of it was that what they were doing seemed more contagious than any disease, and girls from other buses joined in as they all moved toward the door of the school.

Sandy took no active part, but neither did she try to stop what was happening. She knew it would be no use and she might only make the girls turn on her. She walked apart, watching miserably. All this was wrong—but what could she do? Trina was clearly bewildered and angry, but there was no way to get back at her tormentors.

All the way into the classroom the performance was kept up. But after they were in Mr. Wendel's room, the teasing grew more subtle. It amounted to no more than the drawing aside of a skirt as some girl passed Trina's seat, or the snatching away of a dropped pencil that had rolled near her, as though quick action were necessary to avoid becoming contaminated.

Sandy suspected that Mr. Wendel knew something was up since teachers could sense the atmosphere of a class-room quickly. But apparently he could not put a finger on exactly what was happening and he managed to override it in his own way. He made the lesson especially interesting, so that before long everyone was involved in the subject of the hour, and Trina was forgotten for a little while.

At recess it was bad again, and at lunchtime it was worse. This was a small school, without a cafeteria, and the children brought their lunches and ate them in the classrooms. A great deal of whispering and giggling went on around Trina, with the boys watching the girls and talking among themselves about what was happening. Trina could see that by this time Mr. Wendel knew defi-nitely that something was wrong, but apparently he had de-cided to ignore the trouble and to let it die down of its own accord.

Sandy felt disturbed and worried by what she saw. It was clear that an angry reaction was boiling up in Trina. That was something to worry about too, since Sandy had seen Trina fly into a rage. There might be a frightful ex-plosion coming.

Once she leaned toward Melissa in the next seat. "What you're doing doesn't make any sense," she whispered. "Why must you be so mean?"

"Mean?" Melissa widened her eyes at Sandy in exagger-ated innocence. "Do you think we want to catch small-pox-diphtheria-plague?"

Other girls nearby giggled at her words. Only Debra watched from across the room with slightly troubled eyes. She had joined in at first, but now she wasn't enjoying this either. Even if Debra helped her, they wouldn't be strong enough to stop this, Sandy knew.

"Why don't you go and sit with Trina, if you're so brave?" Melissa demanded.

Sandy knew she was not that brave. She didn't want to tease Trina, but neither did she want to be teased. She certainly didn't want to be like Trina, with whom nobody wanted to be friends. Surely the girls would understand that even if she didn't join in this silly game, she wasn't on Trina's side. Goodness knows, Trina didn't want her either.

The afternoon was quieter because everyone was busy, but when school let out for the day, the girls started in again. When Melissa and Sandy went out to the bus, several other girls came along in order to have the fun of teasing Trina up to the last minute. Melissa was especially gruesome.

Sandy found herself walking toward the bus just behind Melissa, with Trina a little way ahead. Mrs. Hellman, who drove the bus, was watching the children come up the steps, but she could not see down into the school yard, where Melissa and her friends were acting up. When Trina started for the bus steps, Melissa began to mimic her awkward gait, limping in an exaggerated manner. Trina did not see, but there was laughter from those watching.

Suddenly, Sandy had stood all she could bear. She was right behind Melissa and she impulsively thrust out with all her might, shoving both hands into Melissa's back. The other girl went down on her knees from the force of the shove, but she was up in an instant, forgetting all about Trina, her eyes dark with anger. She flew at Sandy, punching and kicking violently. Sandy had never been in a fight before, and she tried to pull back from Melissa. All the anger had gone out of her with that one tremendous shove. Now she was helpless to guard herself against Melissa's rough attack.

Then something unexpected happened. A hand caught at Melissa's hair and yanked her around. Another hand shook her roughly with a greater strength than Melissa possessed. Someone slapped her across the face, back and forth, leaving red streaks under stinging blows. Sandy, released, watched helplessly as Trina slapped and shook Melissa. It all happened suddenly, swiftly. Mrs. Hellman started down the bus steps, and from across the yard Mr. Wendel had seen and was running to separate the girls.

Everyone else fell back and the girls who had been watching fled in all directions. Mrs. Hellman held the struggling Melissa, who had red scratches across her face, while Mr. Wendel took a firm hold of Trina.

"This isn't the way to settle anything," he said sternly. "Stop it, Trina. Get hold of yourself."

Trina seemed to go limp in his grasp, and he released her. At once she squirmed away from him, and ran across the school yard toward the town streets. Mr. Wendel looked after her for a moment, and then turned his attention to Melissa and Sandy.

"Perhaps you'd better come into Mrs. Venner's office, girls, so we can find out what this is all about."

Sandy hated that—having to go to the principal's office on her second day in school! But there was nothing else to do. Mrs. Hellman began herding the rest of the children into her bus, and Sandy and Melissa went with Mr. Wendel into the school building. Mr. Wendel walked between them, but now and then Melissa glanced at Sandy with a venomous expression. Any possible friendship Sandy might have had with Melissa and her friends was lost for good. Melissa would never be the forgiving type. Not that Sandy wanted her for a friend anymore. She would rather have no friends at all than be tied to Melissa Morris—even though Melissa's mother was Dad's partner.

The white-haired principal waited behind her desk, watching gravely as Mr. Wendel brought his two charges into her office. She was a tall woman, with bright gray eyes that seemed to see everything, and she had a manner of dignity that made you respect her.

"Sit down, girls," she said, not unkindly, and Melissa and Sandy took a chair at each side of her desk.

For the first time, Sandy realized that she was shaking. Her hands were trembling, her teeth chattering, and she felt ill. Mr. Wendel noticed and brought her a drink of water then put a light hand on her shoulder.

"Here, drink this, Sandy. And relax. We just want to know what happened. Apparently you were watching when Trina and Melissa got into difficulties. Can you tell Mrs. Venner what occurred?"

Sandy found, alarmingly, that she couldn't speak. Her teeth clicked against the rim of the glass, but she managed to swallow some water and it made her feel a little better.

It was Melissa who began to talk. "Watching!" she cried. "Sandra wasn't just watching. She started it. I wasn't doing anything to her—just standing in line to get on the bus, when she ran up and pushed me so hard that I fell."

Mrs. Venner did not raise her voice. "Did you push her, Sandra?"

Sandy could only nod. She was still shaking and her throat felt choked.

"Why did you push?" Mrs. Venner asked in the same quiet voice.

With an effort, Sandy tried to pull herself together. She especially hated to act like this in front of Melissa. And someone had to speak the truth.

"Melissa and the others were teasing Trina. I—I had to make her stop."

"Do you think that was a very good way?" Mrs. Venner asked, her gray eyes solemn.

Sandy was silent. She had not been thinking about how best to handle what was happening. She had simply lost her temper and shoved Melissa. Nor could she be sorry she had.

"What happened next?" Mrs. Venner asked.

"Melissa started to punch me . . ."

"Why wouldn't I punch her?" Melissa demanded. "After what she did to me! I'd have fixed her good too, if it hadn't been for that awful Trina."

Mrs. Venner looked at Mr. Wendel for further explanation. Behind thick lenses his eyes looked serious and a little sad.

"Some of this is my fault, I'm afraid," he admitted. "I knew some sort of trouble was brewing, but instead of finding out what it was, I thought I'd give it a chance to die down—as such things often do. But when it exploded, and I saw Trina slapping Melissa, I ran over and Mrs. Hellman and I pulled them apart. Though not before Trina did some damage." He was looking at Melissa's scratched face, and the bruise that was beginning to show on one cheekbone.

"Yes, I see." Mrs. Venner left her chair and came to examine Melissa's face. "Where is Trina now?"

No one knew. She had simply run off as soon as she could get out of Mr. Wendel's grasp.

"No matter who was to blame," Mrs. Venner went on, "this isn't the way to settle problems. I'm going to ask your mother to come in, Melissa, and Sandy's mother too. We'll need to have a talk about what has happened."

"What about Trina?" Melissa asked crossly.

"I'll speak to her grandmother on the telephone and ask her to bring Trina in with her when she comes to see me tomorrow."

In spite of the trouble she was in, Sandy experienced a twinge of pity for Trina. Her grandmother was going to be angry over this, and she might make everything worse for Trina at home.

Mr. Wendel coughed gently, and Mrs. Venner looked at him.

"I live on Hemlock Road, where the Haineses live," he said. "Perhaps I could talk to Trina's grandparents later today."

"That would be fine." Mrs. Venner nodded and then returned to the matter of the fight.

"This is never the way to settle anything," she repeated. "Don't you agree, Mr. Wendel?"

"Of course I agree," Mr. Wendel said. He stroked a hand thoughtfully over his thinning reddish hair. "Nevertheless, it's a very human way when we lose our tempers."

She gave him a sharp look as though she was not sure whether he was agreeing with her or not.

"Grown-ups fight all the time," Melissa protested. "They even have wars to give them a chance to fight."

"Which doesn't make it any better, or excuse any of us for not working out a better way to settle differences," said Mrs. Venner. "Melissa, we'd better have the nurse look at your face if she's still in the building. How will you girls get home, now that the bus has left?"

"I can take them home," Mr. Wendel offered.

"No, thank you." Melissa was icily polite. "I'll go over to the store and tell my mother what's happened. I'll wait and go home with her."

Sandy's heart dropped another notch. That meant that Dad was going to hear Melissa's version of what had happened first, and she knew that Melissa would play down all the real reasons for the trouble. Dad would probably be awfully mad by the time he got home.

Mr. Wendel moved toward the door. "All right—if you want to do it that way, Melissa. Come along, Sandy, and I'll get you home."

They could hear Mrs. Venner's sigh as they went through the door. It was a sigh Sandy was to remember later.

In the station wagon Mr. Wendel was silent, and Sandy had the uncomfortable feeling that he was disappointed in her. But at least she felt better able to talk now than she had in the principal's office.

"You don't know!" she burst out when he had started the car. "You don't know how awful Melissa was being. And the other girls were following her."

"I can guess." Mr. Wendel said dryly.

"But don't you see—Trina was all alone. And they'd been teasing her all day. She didn't try to fight back until Melissa began to punch me. Then she—she just came to my aid."

In all the excitement and confusion, Sandy had not fully realized the truth of those words. Perhaps Trina had been pretty mad at Melissa on her own, but she hadn't done a thing until she saw Melissa picking on Sandy. So Trina had come to help her.

"It might have been better to call a teacher," Mr. Wendel said gently. "Sometimes things get too big for us to handle alone, and we have to call for outside help."

"There wasn't any time," Sandy said. "It all happened so fast. I didn't think about anything else when I shoved her. Except to make her stop. And I suppose I wanted to hurt her because she was hurting Trina."

"One thing can lead to another," Mr. Wendel said. "I'm sorry it happened."

"I am too," Sandy said gloomily. She had recovered from her shocked, shaky feeling, but now she felt terribly depressed and discouraged. It was awful to have all this trouble right when she was starting in at a new school.

The car had reached the turn-in to Hemlock Road, and Mr. Wendel slowed down.

"Melissa's been having rather a bad time since her father died," he said as they turned into the side road.

"That doesn't excuse her for being horrible to other people," Sandy objected.

"You're perfectly right. It doesn't. But I like to look for reasons behind people's behavior. When I understand why they act as they do, I'm in a better position to deal with such actions. For instance, I can see very well why you pushed Melissa. But why Melissa is so bent on teasing Trina is something a lot more complicated."

Sandy liked the way Mr. Wendel talked. He did not treat his pupils like children who couldn't understand what he was saying. He was speaking to her straight out as if she were a grown-up—the way Dad sometimes did, and as a result she wanted all the more to understand him.

"What do you mean?" she asked. "That is, about why Melissa was teasing Trina."

"She loved her father a great deal," Mr. Wendel went on. "I gather he made a lot of her and let her do almost anything she wanted. I suppose that's not really good for anyone. We all need some rules and limits or we couldn't live together comfortably. Now he's gone—quite suddenly in an accident—and her mother isn't able to manage her. Melissa is unhappy and she doesn't understand what's happening to her. She's perhaps trying to prove to herself that she's as important a person as her father made her believe she was. But like Trina, she's choosing the wrong ways to prove herself."

He had slowed the car at the foot of the Forster drive, and Sandy saw that he was smiling at her as if they were friends. At least he wasn't holding what had happened against her.

"Do you want me to take you up to the house?" he asked. "Or would you rather walk up the drive by yourself?"

He understood about that too, she thought gratefully. If she was brought home in Mr. Wendel's car, Mother would ask questions, and she would have to stop and tell her the whole story and discuss everything. She wanted to do that. Mother would listen and understand. But right now there was no time, because she must do something else first. Something important. The idea had begun to grow in her mind as Mr. Wendel talked. Now she had to decide what to do.

She thanked the teacher and got out of the car. He said, "Don't worry—things will work out. They always do when people really try."

Sandy watched him turn the car around and drive off down the road. Then she started slowly up the drive.

When people really try, he had said. But Melissa wasn't

trying to work things out. And neither was Trina—and perhaps not Sandy Forster. She felt increasingly troubled and confused.

As she climbed the curving driveway, she noticed for the first time that the afternoon had turned gray, and that a cloud bank was rising beyond the Gap. The air had grown colder too, so perhaps it was going to snow again.

But never mind the weather. Now she must decide whether it was possible for *her* to do one right thing. The thought that had come to her was simply that she knew where Trina was. She knew very well where she would have gone. And now Sandy felt that she must talk to her. She must talk to her even before she told her mother all that had happened. At that moment she wanted her mother's comfort and counsel quite urgently—but she knew the matter of Trina could not wait.

When she reached the house she ran inside and called out, "I'm home! But I have to go up in the woods before I do anything else. Is that okay, Mother? I'll come back soon."

Her mother came to the front door, where Sandy was putting down her books. With one look she recognized her daughter's urgency.

"All right," she said. "If something has happened, you can tell me about it when you get back. But stay on the paths you know, and don't get lost."

"I won't," Sandy promised, and ran out the door and toward the trail that led up the mountain.

7

Rising Storm

Woods and trail looked different this time. Snow under the trees had not melted up here on the mountain where it was colder than in the valley town. It lay white and untrampled on all sides. Sandy could see deeply into the woods because of the contrast between white earth and brown tree trunks. White aisles stretched away in every direction, where before everything has blurred together in earth and brush that was all of one color. Now anything that moved in there among the trees would be clearly visible.

The trail, however, was not entirely unmarked. The prints of a pair of boots marched straight up the hill and around the turns in the path. Trina had gone this way, as Sandy had been sure she would. She would want to escape the school and the town, and she would not go straight home to face her grandmother's indignation, now that she was in trouble. There was just one hiding place she would know might welcome her.

Sandy walked quickly, partly to keep from changing her mind and partly because of a cold wind blowing at her back. The gray bank of clouds was moving swiftly overhead, and the very air had begun to feel stormy.

In spite of what she was doing, however, she did not really want to talk to Trina. She only knew she must. Trina had come to her aid and made Melissa stop punching her. She owed her something for that. She owed it, even if Trina might be the first to reject such payment.

Her boots crunched into the snow as she walked, leaving another line of prints beside Trina's. Sometimes animal tracks led across the path—tracks of all sizes that she had no way of identifying. There were tiny, birdlike scratches on the surface, while other marks were deeper and larger, but all were individually patterned, and meant that something live had walked on the snow. It would be fun to find out which animals had made each track, but she could not stop to study them now.

When she reached the rise in the hill, before it dipped
down into the hollow, she saw blue woodsmoke curling
up between the trees. That would be smoke from the
chimney of the cabin. So Trina was there and she had
lighted a fire.

Her foot tracks led down the hill right to the cabin door.
Sandy followed them and saw that smoke puffed steadily
from the stone chimney as she paused before the cabin
door. She felt more uncertain than ever, and even a little
fearful. Trina was not one to welcome intrusion, and just
because she had come to Sandy's aid did not mean they
were friends. Trina wanted no friends and she would probably resent having Sandy follow her to the cabin.

She thought of going around to look in a window in order to see what Trina was doing, but she rejected that. It
wasn't fair to spy. But neither could she walk straight in
the door. She went up to it and knocked hesitantly.

There was silence from within. She called out, "It's
Sandy. Will you let me come in?"

For a moment longer the silence held. Then Trina said,
"What for?" and she sounded anything but hospitable.

Oddly enough, at that moment Sandy remembered Mrs.
Venner's sigh. She knew how the principal had felt.

"I want to tell you what happened," she called. "I'll go
away quickly."

"The door isn't locked," Trina said, and Sandy knew that
was as close to an invitation as Trina would come. She
opened the door and walked into a room that had begun
to lose its chill, thanks to the flaming wood that crackled
in the fireplace.

Trina had taken off her coat, and she still wore her
school clothes—a yellow checked dress that looked decep-
tively bright and cheerful in the gray light of the cabin.
She was sitting in one of the straight chairs pulled up to
the wooden table, and open before her was her shoe box
of treasures. A knitted yellow tam-o'-shanter sat squarely
upon her winter-leaf hair, but to spoil the bright effect she
wore a deep scowl on her forehead.

"Hello," Sandy said, closing the door behind her. "That
fire looks good. Do you mind if I get warm?"

Trina shrugged, and Sandy went over to the fire, pulled
off her mittens, stuffing them into a coat pocket, and held
her cold fingers out to the blaze.

"What do you want?" Trina said after a while.

"You—you stopped Melissa from hitting me," Sandy said. Though she didn't mean it that way, the words came out sounding like an accusation.

"So what?" Trina was curt, anything but friendly.

Sandy turned around and walked toward the table. Without asking if she might, she sat down in the opposite chair. Then, without choosing her words too carefully, because they seemed to just pop into her mind, she told Trina what had happened after she had run away.

The other girl listened without being impressed. "You didn't need to come and tell me all that," Trina said, when she finished. "It's just the same old thing. The office and Mrs. Venner and somebody blaming me for everything."

"Maybe it wasn't just like that," Sandy said. "I mean— they blamed me for starting it. Mrs. Venner said I shouldn't have shoved Melissa, and she shouldn't have hit me, and you shouldn't have finished up by hitting her. So we're all to blame."

Trina was staring in a strangely unfamiliar way. Suddenly Sandy realized that the other girl had begun to laugh. She wasn't scowling anymore, and her green eyes were dancing with amusement—something Sandy had never seen in them before.

"It sure was funny, the way it happened," Trina said. "Everybody pushing and hitting—and Melissa getting the worst of it. I'll bet I fixed up her face real good. She won't look so pretty for a while. Now maybe she'll let me alone."

"Anyway, I'm glad you helped me," Sandy said. "I never got into a fight with anybody before. I—I didn't like it."

"Then you'd better not go shoving people in the first place," Trina said. She regarded Sandy with mild curiosity. "Why did you, anyway?"

"Why—because she was teasing you, of course. She'd been doing it all day. I thought it was mean and I couldn't stand it anymore. I got mad and gave her a good shove."

This time Trina looked surprised. "But you were there with Melissa and the others all the time. I thought you were teasing me too."

"I did, once," Sandy admitted. "But not after that time with the ball. I didn't do the other things they were doing."

"At lunch you sat with them."

"My seat is next to Melissa's—how could I help it? But I was trying to get her to stop."

Trina looked disbelievingly. "Why would you do that? You don't like me."

"You don't give anybody a chance to like you. You've been mad at me ever since I came."

Trina thought about that for a moment. "Well—I didn't want you to come. I wanted these woods to belong to me."

"Because they don't belong to you doesn't mean you can't use them all you want to. You weren't even friendly when Cliff brought me over to your grandfather's workshop yesterday. Just the same, you've helped me twice. You kept me from being lost in the woods all night, and you stopped Melissa from punching me. When you help people, you owe them something."

Trina looked startled. "Owe them something? Why?"

Sandy was not entirely sure herself. It was a thought that had just come to her. "You ought to be able to figure that out. You're not stupid."

"Some people think I am," Trina said.

They sat at the table for a few minutes staring at each other. Then Trina almost smiled. Smiling was probably harder for her than laughing, since in her laughter there was always scorn.

"In that case you owe me something too," she said. "Because you helped me."

Sandy nodded, and they grinned at each other. Sandy was beginning to understand her own idea a little better. When you helped someone, you took on a responsibility toward her. Having pulled her out of trouble, you had a feeling that you wanted to keep her out—whether you liked it or not. If you saved a person from something, you didn't want her to rush right back into trouble.

She decided to press her advantage in the face of Trina's unexpected grin.

"What are we going to do about that committee Mr. Wendel put us on?" she asked. "How can we ever work it out with Melissa and Debra and Ginger in the same group? How can we work together?"

Trina's laughter was scornful again. "We won't, of course. Don't you think I know what Mr. Wendel's trying to do? He's trying to show those girls how much I know. As if I cared!"

"Why don't you care?" Sandy asked softly.

Trina stared at her. "Why should I? Do you think I need them? Do *you* need them?"

"I don't like being alone," Sandy said. "In New York I had lots of friends. Here I haven't any."

For a few moments Trina was silent. She left the table and went to look out a window into the woods. Sandy heard a clatter against the windowpanes, as if someone had tossed a handful of sand.

"It's sleeting," Trina said. "It can get cold fast up here on the mountain. There may be an ice storm coming."

Sandy joined her at the window. The sleet looked wet and unpleasant and it would sting her face when she walked into it, she thought, shivering.

"Can we wait until it stops before we leave?" she asked.

Trina went to examine the fire. "It's burning down. I didn't put on much wood because I don't like to leave a fire burning when I'm not here to watch it. We can wait until it's down to embers, and then I'll put it out with water."

After that neither girl said anything for a time. Sandy felt no more comfortable with Trina than she had before. She had no idea what to talk about. But when Trina came to the table and sat down, Sandy joined her again.

Trina seemed to be thinking, and after a while she drew the shoe box toward her and poked among the objects in the box. Then she took out the square plaque of wood with its carving of leaves and tiny, bell-shaped flowers.

"That's lily of the valley," she said, pushing the carving toward Sandy. "My mother said it was her favorite flower, so she carved this for me. She always used to wear lily-of-the-valley perfume. That's what was in this bottle. You can still smell it."

She took the stopper from the bottle and held the bit of glass out to Sandy, who bent to sniff. A faint, sweet perfume still clung to the stopper, though the bottle was empty.

"It smells nice," Sandy said, sensing that in opening this box Trina had come as close to an offer of friendship as she could make.

"The next time I have some money to spend," Trina said dreamily, "I'm going to buy some lily-of-the-valley perfume."

Somehow perfume did not seem to go with Trina the way she usually looked.

The next object she drew from the box was the rusty penknife.

"That belonged to my dad. It was about the only thing he left behind. Mother kept it, and Lucy found it in her things after she died. She threw it away, but I took it out of the trash and kept it."

"Lucy?" Sandy said.

"Sure. Lucy and Sam. My grandparents."

"Do they let you call them by their first names?"

"How can they stop me? Lucy hates it. That's why I do it. Sam doesn't care. Sam would be okay if Lucy didn't run him. I think he goes out in his workshop to get away from her chatter. The way I come up here in the woods."

The next object Trina took out of the box was the shabby strawberry pincushion. She poked at it with a curious finger.

"I made that for my mother when I was in kindergarten, and she kept it. It's hard to remember back that far. It's as though I was somebody else then." She touched the packet that held the snapshot, but did not pick it up. "Just the way it seems I must have been someone else in this picture. I don't remember my mother as pretty as this. Neither can I remember her the way she looked in that picture Lucy keeps in the living room."

Sandy could find nothing to say, but she could imagine how she would feel if she were in Trina's place, if it were her own mother who was gone. The very thought made tears burn behind her eyes. She blinked hard, because she knew Trina would hate having someone feel sorry for her.

"I've never showed these things to anybody else," Trina said. She watched Sandy, her green eyes strangely alert, as though she waited for something she might pounce upon.

"Thank you for showing me," Sandy said awkwardly. She wished she could like Trina better. She wished the faint feeling of distrust would go away.

Trina put everything back and covered the box. When she had hidden it away in the drawer, she poured water from a plastic jug onto the remains of the fire, and carefully stirred around in the embers with a poker until she was satisfied the fire was out. The cabin was already growing colder, and she put on her coat.

"We'd better leave pretty soon. It may be icy out there.

Sometimes it's hard to walk when it freezes right after rain or sleet."

Sandy had kept on her outdoor things and she started for the door, but Trina stopped her before she opened it.

"You were talking about that committee Mr. Wendel put us on with Melissa and the other two. Maybe it will work out all right."

A faint feeling of hope began to stir in Sandy. After what had happened in school today, she had begun to dread the idea of the committee.

"If only you'd try to help——" she began.

Trina's smile was not altogether reassuring. "I'm going to. I know what I can do. For once I'm going to get the best marks in the class. And I'll help you to get a good mark too. That is, if you're really on my side."

Sandy stared at her doubtfully. "Why must there be sides? Why can't we all work together?"

"Like Brotherhood and all that sort of thing?" Trina snorted unpleasantly. "Do you think Melissa is going to want to work with us after what happened today?"

"She'll have to, won't she? I mean Mr. Wendel, and Mrs. Venner, and maybe even her mother——"

"She'll pretend to work with us," Trina said, "because she likes to get good marks. But we're going to fix that between us. And I know just how we can do it."

"What do you mean?" Sandy asked, feeling uncomfortable all over again.

"Just wait and see. I'll figure it out. I think I know what we can do. Come on—let's get started down the hill."

Sandy went first and waited outside until Trina had closed the cabin door. It was still sleeting, and overhead the trees had begun to droop under their fresh weight of ice. All around, the woods seemed to creak and murmur as the wind rushed among the tall trunks. Sandy wondered where the animals hid when there was a storm.

"Trina—did you really see a bear up here?" she asked abruptly.

"I didn't see one. Though I think there might be one around. I just wanted to scare you the other day."

"But if there's one around——"

"He won't bother us. Wild animals stay away from people. Come along."

The crunchy surface of the snow, which had been easy to walk on, had iced over with a slick and slippery coating. Sandy took several steps before both feet flew out from under her. She thumped down on the path with a jar that hurt all the way through. Trina, stepping more carefully because she was aware of the danger, stood looking down at her, laughing.

It took a few tries for Sandy to scramble to her feet, with Trina offering no help and laughing harder than ever. When she had recovered her balance, she faced the other girl angrily.

"You know what's the matter with you? You're awfully busy being sorry for Trina Carpozi, but you think it's funny when somebody else gets hurt. Do *you* like to be laughed at? Don't you know that other people have feelings?"

Trina gave her an odd look and went ahead on the path without answering. Sandy followed grumpily, watching where the other girl stepped, setting her feet down carefully. When she could, Trina walked on brown grass at the side of the trail, where she could get a foothold, or she stepped on high spots that had shed the sleet and had not yet iced over. The wind was blowing harder than ever, and ice particles stung their faces as they headed downhill. Now and then Sandy took hold of a tree trunk in order to get over some especially slick place, and once, to her surprise, Trina stopped on the far side of a big ice patch to help her across.

Getting back to the house took longer than usual, and lights were shining through the dusk when they came out of the woods. The grass around the house was rough to walk on, but it wasn't slippery because every blade stood up stiffly, encrusted with ice that cracked under their weight as they stepped on it. They made a great clatter walking across the lawn.

Mother heard them coming and opened the door. "Hello, girls. I was getting worried. You both look frozen. Trina, come in by the fire and warm up before you go home. Your grandmother's been phoning."

Trina groaned as she got out of her coat and boots, and Sandy realized that if Mrs. Haines had phoned, it probably meant that Mr. Wendel had been to see her and that she knew what had happened at school. And probably she'd told it to Sandy's mother.

"I've had a call from your father too, Sandy," Mother went on. "Suppose you girls go in by the fire, and I'll make some hot chocolate. Then you can both tell me about what happened. I seem to be getting assorted versions."

Trina gave Sandy a sidelong look as they went into the living room, where Mother had built a good fire in the grate.

"There's time for us to fix up a good story," she said.

Sandy stared at her. "But our story is fixed up. We can tell Mother exactly what happened. She'll listen and she'll try to understand."

"Grown-ups never understand," Trina said bluntly. "We can make it much worse for Melissa. You can say you never shoved her, and I'll back you up. Then they won't know who to believe."

"You like to make trouble, don't you?" Sandy said.

Trina's sly grin seemed to indicate that she felt this was a compliment. "Why not?" she challenged. "Everybody makes trouble for me."

That was true. There was no use talking to her. Sandy sat cross-legged on the hearthrug before the fire. This was a bigger, better blaze than the one up in the cabin, and she tried to stop her racing thoughts by watching pictures in the flames. Trina sat on a hassock, farther away from the radiating heat. She had returned to her usual sullen state, staring at nothing, looking a little stupid. But Sandy knew now that she wasn't stupid. She was clever about making a perfectly horrible life for herself. Only she wasn't quite clever enough to see what she was doing.

Mother came in to set a tray on the coffee table she pulled over to the fire. The hot chocolate, whipped to a froth, wore a bubbly cinnamon foam on top, and steam rose enticingly from pink-and-brown mugs. Sandy picked up her mug and sipped the warm sweetness. Then she nibbled on an oatmeal cooky from the plate on the tray. It was a moment when food was comforting.

Not even Trina could resist the invitation of a hot drink. When both girls had finished part of their chocolate, and the cookies had diminished on the plate, Mother pulled a chair close to the fire and clasped her hands about her knees. She had put on trim brown slacks and a green-and-yellow sweater that had come from Norway.

"Who'd like to tell me the story?" she asked.

Mother never went into a flap, the way Dad sometimes

did, and Sandy decided it would be better to get all this over before Dad came home.

Trina opened her mouth, but before she could say whatever she intended, Sandy burst in with an account of what had happened and what had led up to the shove she had given Melissa. Once or twice when Trina tried to break in, Sandy simply raised her voice and talked faster. She admitted blame for the push, and she gave credit to Trina for coming to her aid when Melissa had been trying to hurt her. But she also admitted that Trina had been too rough, and that a teacher should have been called on the scene to help earlier.

Mother's blue eyes caught the reflection of dancing flames as she listened, not saying anything. She looked concerned, but not in the least disbelieving. Sandy could always talk straight to her. Right at the end of the story, Dad came stamping in, out of temper and in one of his best flaps.

The thing he was upset about, however, was the ice storm. Snow tires didn't help much on ice. The highway was being sanded, but the side road hadn't been sanded as yet, and he had slid off into a ditch, having to leave the car where it was while he got out and walked home.

"At least it's off the road," he said. "Nobody will hit it, and tomorrow I'll get it towed out. But I practically had to skate home the rest of the way—our drive is a sheet of ice. I came up the hill over the grass."

"Would you like some hot chocolate?" Mother asked soothingly.

Dad shook his head. "Hot coffee, please. Use instant, so I can have it fast." He gave one last sigh of exasperation and dropped into his own easy chair. For the first time he seemed to notice Trina and Sandy. "Ha!" he said. "The conspirators! I understand you two turned the school upside down today. Nice going, Sandy, when I'm trying to make a hit with the people who live here."

Mother had gone back to the kitchen and didn't hear, so Sandy was left to deal with this on her own. "It was bad enough," she said, "but maybe Melissa made it even worse."

Dad grunted. "She had a scratched face to show for what happened, and I gather that both you and Trina jumped her and started to beat her up."

Trina snorted, and Sandy made a gasping sound.

"Not a word of which do I believe," Dad went on. "I suspect from the way Melissa talked that she wasn't quite the angel she was trying to make out to her mother."

Sandy felt like hugging him. "What did her mother say?"

"I'm afraid she believed all of it. She cried a little and hoped that you and Trina would be severely punished. I told her I'd have to hear your story and Trina's first."

In spite of herself, Sandy giggled. She was feeling better by the moment. When she glanced at Trina she saw that she was gaping at Dad in surprise.

Mother came back with the hot coffee. "We'll have to decide what to do," she said, joining them at the fire. "In a minute, Ted, I'll tell you all about it. I imagine Sandy's tired of going over the same ground. Though we'd like to hear what Trina has to say too. Of course I'll go and talk to Mrs. Venner at school, and see if I can cooperate in smoothing things out. By this time Sandy realizes that she went too far and tried to handle what Melissa was doing in the wrong way. And while I'm glad that Trina tried to help Sandy, I expect she also realizes that to slap Melissa and scratch her face wasn't the best solution."

"No, it wasn't," Trina said defiantly. "Next time I'll hurt her more if she doesn't leave me alone."

"Would you like to tell us what happened, as you see it?" Mother asked gently.

Trina made a further sound of disgruntlement, threw a puzzled look at Sandy, and then subsided. "Sandy's told you what happened. That's the way it was," she said grudgingly.

Mother nodded and stood up. "I wanted to make sure before I called your grandmother. I'll go phone her now. How would you like to stay here with Sandy tonight? It's going to be difficult to get down that slippery hill in the dark, and we haven't a car, even if we could get it up and down the driveway."

Trina had turned slightly pink, and she looked as though she had lost all power of speech. Whatever response she had expected from her defiance, it wasn't this. Sandy, however, could not feel happy about the plan, though she could see it might give Trina's grandmother a little time to cool off.

"What about it, Trina?" Mother said. "Would you like to stay?"

Obviously, Trina was not used to being obliging, and her confusion and mixed impulses showed in her face. At least she had stopped being sullen. Mother reached over and gave her a light pat on the shoulder.

"Never mind. You don't have to put it into words, unless you'd rather go home. It's always fun to stay overnight in other people's houses."

"I've never stayed overnight in anybody's house," Trina said. She picked up her cup of chocolate and drained the last drops with a slurping sound.

Mother went off to phone, and there was quiet in the room. Outside, sleet clattered against the picture windows, and Sandy was glad she was not out in that weather. This was going to be a long night. Somehow she could not look forward to it. How was she to endure Trina for that length of time?

As Dad drank his coffee and the two girls stared into the fire, the lights in the room flared brightly, dipped to a pinpoint, and slowly faded out. From the direction of the telephone Mother gave a little shriek. Firelight lent the room a soft glow as Dad rose to his feet.

"That does it," he said. "That's all we need. Probably there's an icy branch down over a line someplace. And if I know the country, it may be a while before we have lights again. I suppose you know what that means?"

"Sure," Trina said, experienced in such matters. "It means no light, no heat, no stove, and pretty quickly, with the pump stopped, no running water."

Sandy jumped up from the hearthrug. "I know where the candles are. I'll get some and light them." Unreasonably, she felt more cheerful—even a little excited. Other troubles could be forgotten in the face of a new adventure.

Mother came back to the room, groping her way. "Thank goodness the telephone still works. It's all right, Trina. Your grandmother says you can stay for the night. Her lights have gone out too."

A few moments later the phone rang and it was Mrs. Wendel, checking to see if the Forsters had lost electric power.

All Hemlock Road was dark.

8

Blackout

Red and green Christmas candles, brought out ahead of time, were set on the mantel, on a coffee table, on top of a bookcase in the living room. In the kitchen Mother worked by the light of several white candle stubs, saved when the dining room candles burned down.

By great good luck, she had been cooking a stew well before dinner. It was piping hot and had cooked long enough to be eaten, so they had a hot dinner by candle-light in the kitchen, with huge soup plates of stew, delicious with beef, onions, potatoes, and carrots.

The refrigerator was off, of course, but the salad greens were still crisp, and both girls had glasses of cold milk with their stew. Because Mother had been heating water for Dad's coffee a little while before, there was still hot water in the kettle, and she and Dad could have almost-hot instant coffee.

Dad remembered there was a wood-burning stove in the garage, and he went out to light a fire in it and put a kettle and a big pan of water on to heat. This was a slow way to get boiling water, but it would work in time. If it was necessary, tomorrow Mother could warm canned foods and leftovers on the garage stove. At least Dad had had the forethought, when they moved in, to store several jugs of water against emergency. In the country the water pump that served the well could fail at times.

He had also phoned the electric company, which was swamped with calls. Apparently wires were down everywhere because of the ice storm, and the most populated areas had to be taken care of first. So it might be a while before the work crews got out to Hemlock Road.

"This happens every once in a while," Trina told them. "The tree crews have to come through cutting down whatever's leaning against the wires and chopping out branches that could fall later. When that's done, they call in the inspection men. After all the wires have been checked, the inspection men get in touch with the place where the main power is turned on. Then we can have light. If it's real bad in a lot of places, it may be a long time before we get electricity again."

Nobody grumbled, however, even when the house began to grow cold. Mother piled the dishes in the sink, to wait until the water could be turned on. She put the remainder of the cooled stew away in the refrigerator, which would take a while to warm up. Then they all gathered in the living room, where Dad kept the fire alive with logs Mr. Seale had cut from fallen trees in the woods.

Sandy got out a checkerboard and she and Trina sat before the fire playing checkers in the flickering light. Shadows danced on the ceiling, and sometimes, when a log flared up in the grate, the room grew almost bright, only to fall into dimness again as the wood burned down. Candle flames stood straight as arrows, only swaying with currents of air when someone moved about the room.

Mother and Dad talked quietly together, but no one mentioned what had happened in school that day. Trina did not even ask what her grandmother had said on the phone. She was a good checker player—she played often with Sam, she said—and Sandy had trouble winning a single game. As the house grew colder, everyone put on extra sweaters and found it wasn't wise to move very far from the fireplace. Fortunately, the temperature was only just below freezing outside, so it was not bitterly cold.

A moment came when everyone was silent in the living room. Sandy's head was bent over the checkerboard as she planned her next move—right after Trina had jumped two men, including a king. Dad was trying to read newspaper headlines by candlelight, and Mother sat with her head back in her chair, just thinking.

Because everything was still, the footsteps outside sounded crackling loud on the frozen grass. Everyone started and stared toward the picture windows, where candle reflections shone in the black glass. Who could be walking out there? Who on earth could have braved the icy road and still icier hill in the darkness?

Quietly they all got up and moved to the big windows. With her back to the candles, Sandy found that she could see moonlight shining on a crystal world. As they watched, a doe and two fawns came crackling across the grass beside the house and looked curiously through the windows, interested in the candlelit scene. It was a lovely moment, while wild creatures and human creatures stared at each other, with no challenge between them, and no fright. Sandy had a choked feeling in her throat because she was a part of something so wonderful. This was happening to *her*.

"We're lucky," Dad said softly. "We're lucky to be in time to have an experience like this. If the country isn't careful, after a while there will be no places where the wild things can come. There'll be too many people, too many highways, too much concrete, too many housing developments. All this will be gone—as it's going, even now."

The doe pricked up her ears—probably at the sound of Dad's voice—but still she did not take fright. The two fawns paid no attention, having no experience with men who might hunt them. They nosed into the evergreen shrubbery that grew close to the house, nibbling at the tenderest growth, sampling the red berries of a firethorn bush.

"There go our bushes," Dad said, but Mother shook her head. "I'd rather have the deer. We can always grow new bushes."

For a little while longer the mother deer and her children fed just outside the windows. Then an icy branch crashed to earth in the nearby woods, and all three flung up their white tails and went leaping away across the frozen grass, adding their own clatter to the crash of ice. It was beautiful to see their graceful leaps, and everyone watched until they were lost among the trees.

When they had gone, the glittering ice world lay still and empty in the moonlight, and the night was hushed. Mother and Dad went back to their chairs, but Sandy and Trina stayed at the window, held by the magic out there. The storm was over and there were bright stars in the sky, and the same round, glowing moon up there that men from earth had walked upon.

Looking at the moon, Sandy thought, as she often did, of that night back in the city when she had been allowed to stay up to watch a moon landing on television. Through their apartment windows that night, they had been able to see the moon in the sky at the same time that men from earth were landing upon it—men who could be seen on a picture screen, moving about awkwardly on the ancient, dusty surface. They had been filled with wonder that night, watching the real moon and the picture on television at the same time.

But there were wonders on earth too, and Sandy knew she had been part of one tonight. Now, though the hills and woods were quiet, she was aware that if a camera could move among the trees, it would photograph an infinite variety of wildlife. Insects and tiny animals such as mice and moles, and larger animals such as raccoons and woodchucks and even foxes, would be moving about out there in the darkness. For the first time she began to sense the country about her in a new way. Not as something strange and hostile, but as a new life opening to take her in. Her feeling about the city had faded just a little.

On a distant ridge lights glowed in homes not touched by the blackout. And once, very close to the window, a rabbit, silhouetted against the ice, went bounding across the lawn.

"Lippety, lippety, lippety," said Sandy, smiling.

At her side, Trina caught her breath. "That's how Peter Rabbit ran! When I was little my father used to read me that story."

The sharing of an almost forgotten *Peter Rabbit* and the wonderment of the universe made a difference in how she felt about Trina too, Sandy thought. For a little while there was a sense of understanding between them.

After the deer and the rabbit, checkers seemed rather a bore, and when they returned to the game, Sandy let Trina win quickly. Then she folded up the board and put the red and black counters away in their box. This seemed a good time for talking, and as they sat there with the fire and candles making a soft glow around them, Dad began to ask Trina questions about Mr. Seale and the building of the pond. Trina knew all about this, and Sandy listened with surprised interest. She had not realized Trina could talk like this. These were things Sandy would need to know for the ecology project at school, so she might as well learn them while she had a chance. She could not be certain that Trina would tell her all this later when she was in a different mood. And she would probably never tell Melissa and her friends.

Trina explained that the United States Conservation Service wanted to encourage the preservation of water. They employed men who were experts on the building of ponds, men who would examine one's property and make all the plans for a pond, even supervising its building, without any charge to the owner. Of course, Mr. Seale had to pay for the actual digging of the pond and the building of the dam.

"They tested the ground out there," Trina said. "One of the Conservation men showed where he wanted holes dug to make certain there would be enough water. He also examined the earth to be sure the dam would hold water. Then they picked the best place for the pond to be built, and a contractor came in with a bulldozer and dug out the pond. Since one side of the area sloped away, a big dam had to be built to hold the water in, and extra earth had to be brought down to make the dam."

"Where did they get the earth?" Dad asked.

"Up in the woods. The Conservation men picked a section that had to be cleared of trees, and the earth was brought down from that section. That's what they call 'borrow.' "

Sandy remembered the bare place she had seen up in the woods.

"Did they have to cut down many trees?" Mother asked.

"Yes, hundreds of them—a whole acre or more, but a lot of those trees were trashy growth that didn't matter too much. Mr. Seale made sure the contractor saved an entire hemlock grove up there, near where he wanted earth. And there's one big pine tree near the road that wasn't cut down. Now the Conservation Service will show you how to plant new trees to cover the raw place. Trees make the air better to breathe because they give out oxygen."

This was all fascinating, and Sandy found herself listening to Trina with increasing surprise. She hardly seemed like the same girl now that she was talking of the things she knew and cared about most.

"Mr. Seale told me he'd had a forester up there in another part of the woods," Dad said, "to mark the trees that should be weeded out. These will be cut down so that the more desirable trees will have a better chance. That's why there are spray-paint marks on a lot of trees up there. I want to continue the program he started. Forests can be improved by care."

The next sound from outdoors that broke in upon them was the rumble of a truck. They all rushed to the windows again and saw headlights down the road. Two trucks had stopped near the foot of the drive, and men in hard hats were busy with spotlight beams, working among the broken branches of trees. One of the vehicles was a "cherry picker"—with a basket that could be elevated so a man could stand in it and reach high sections of a tree. It was fun to watch them for a while, but even this activity grew tiresome eventually—and there were still no lights.

By ten o'clock Mother said it was bed as usual, blackout or not. Dad went out to tend the stove in the garage and bring in hot water for washing and to fill hot-water bottles. A cot for Trina was put up in Sandy's bedroom, and Mother found two hot-water bags, and a rubber ice bag that could be used for hot water, and tucked them into all the beds.

Sandy and Trina undressed before the fire, and Trina put on a pair of Sandy's pajamas that were a little tight for her. The bedroom was cold, and as Sandy walked into it she tried automatically to turn on the light. Mother and Dad had been doing the same thing all evening—it was a difficult habit to break. The bed sheets were icy as the two girls got into their separate beds with squeals of dismay. Sandy's cold feet sought the wonderful warmth of the hot-water bottle at the foot of the bed, wrapped in a towel so it wouldn't burn her. She pulled it up to hug it to her, trying to absorb its warmth.

Mother had brought in a candle when she came to tuck them in, and she set down a flashlight on the table beside Sandy's bed.

"This is how everyone used to live," she reminded them. "Often in the country only the living room and the kitchen were heated by hearth fires or a stove. People were supposed to get into cold beds and get up in icy rooms. So think about that."

"It's s-s-sort of f-f-fun," Sandy said between chattering teeth.

Trina made no comment.

Usually Jenny Forster kissed her daughter good night before she turned out the light and went away, but tonight she did not bend over Sandy's bed. She simply gave each girl an affectionate pat, then carried the candle away, leaving them in darkness. Sandy knew why. Trina did not know her mother well enough to be kissed, and Mother didn't want to make any difference between them.

"Such a funny sort of day," Sandy whispered, when her mother had gone, taking away the candle. "So many different things seemed to happen today. I wonder what tomorrow will be like."

Trina's answer came in a voice as soft as her own. "I wish it could stay like this."

"It never can," Sandy sighed. "But I expect it would get tiresome if everything was always the same."

"Tomorrow there's school," Trina said. "And my grandmother, and Melissa, and all that awful mess. I wish I could run away into the woods and never come out."

"That wouldn't help much," Sandy said. She felt like asking who had made everything such a mess anyway, but she did not speak the words. True, Melissa had teased Trina, but before that Trina had undoubtedly done everything she could to invite teasing. And perhaps that was because of what circumstances and people had, in turn, done to Trina. The chain seemed endless. But somewhere along the line somebody had to stop what was happening. She—Sandy Forster—could have managed better if she hadn't lost her temper and pushed Melissa.

And then—in contrary fashion, right while she was thinking all these sensible thoughts—the memory of that moment when they were in line to board the school bus returned to her. She could remember the cruel way Melissa had called Trina "Clumpy," and had mimicked her walk. She could remember vividly the moment when she had pushed Melissa. That moment of angry satisfaction. Laughter bubbled in her throat—soft laughter that broke the silence.

Trina was alert at once. "What's so funny?"

"I was thinking of when I pushed Melissa," Sandy whispered. "You know something—I'm glad I did!"

Trina laughed too. "And I'm glad I slapped her. Tomorrow it will be even better. Because I know the way to get even with her. We'll do it together. Tomorrow I'll show you the way."

All tendency to laugh was suddenly gone. Sandy had had her moment, but she didn't want any more of this. She wanted it to stop. She couldn't go on pushing people. Now Melissa would want to get even, and Trina still wanted that. This was the way it went. And everybody ran around in unhappy circles.

"I don't want to get even with anybody," she protested. "Why can't we just go to school tomorrow and be nice to

Melissa and the other girls? So they won't have any excuse
to be against us."

"Do you think that would work?" Trina said impatiently. "Melissa would be just the same. You don't think
she's going to like me any better now, do you? Or you, either. There's nothing we can do to make her like us, any
more than we like her. It's the same with my grandmother.
She hated my father, and she won't ever let me forget it.
That's why I named the little dog I rescued after my father. So I could say, 'Charlie, Charlie,' all the time, and
my grandmother couldn't stop me. Though she only calls
him 'it' or 'you.' She didn't want me to keep Charlie, but
Sam said I could. And sometimes when Sam puts down
his foot she has to go along."

"Where did you get—Charlie?" Sandy asked.

"I found him out on the highway. A car hit him and
broke his leg. He'd have died if I hadn't brought him
home. Sam helped me set the bone, and he got well, even
though he limps. I can't walk so good either, so that
makes us pals."

Trina's voice was gentler than Sandy had ever heard it,
and she considered the strange, rather unhappy fact that
Trina loved Charlie more than she did anything else. More
than she did any person.

They did not talk after that, and before long both girls
fell asleep.

Then, quite suddenly, at two o'clock in the morning
Sandy wakened to find lights burning full on in the room.
The power was back! She sat up in bed and smiled happily
at the warm, golden glow. How bright electricity was, and
what a yellow light it made! She would appreciate it a
little more from now on.

Trina lay sleeping soundly, undisturbed, and Sandy
wondered if she should waken her to share the miracle.
But she decided against it. Asleep, all the sullen, defiant
lines were smoothed out of Trina's face, and she looked
very young and defenseless. It was better to let her sleep.
Sandy got out of bed in the cold and turned off the light.
Downstairs in the basement she could hear the wonderful
sound of the furnace running. It was fun to have a different sort of experience—but she preferred modern con-
veniences. She did not really want to go back to the old
way of living.

When she next awakened it was morning, and she found

Trina up and looking out of the window at the birch grove.

"Come and see," Trina said, when she realized that Sandy was awake.

Sandy stood beside her at the window. The sun was out and the world glittered with ice. All the slender birch trees were arched over, weighted down with their icy burden, their heads frozen to the ground. Their branches and twigs made a lacework of rainbow colors as sunlight struck the shining surfaces. Beyond the birch tree arches, sturdier forest trees towered, equally frozen as they reached stiffly toward the sky, with broken branches hanging down here and there. Everywhere the frozen grass of the lawn was rough with a curious green ice, because of the color that still lingered underneath from summertime.

"A storm like that does a lot of damage," Trina said. "The trees are weakened by all that heavy ice, and when the wind blows they can break. Look—it's beginning to snow."

Even as they watched, great flakes began drifting down from a cloud moving across the sun. The Gap and the distant hills were quickly blotted from sight. But though the rainbows vanished, the white ice world remained, and slowly, softly, snow began to blanket all the burdened trees.

"No school today!" Trina cried in triumph. "Too much ice. And now maybe a blizzard."

Sandy felt a great load of dread slip from her shoulders. The trouble could be postponed. It could all be put off until tomorrow—or the next day.

"Let's get dressed," she said.

The room was warm and they dressed quickly, taking turns in the bathroom. Then they went out to where the smell of bacon filled the kitchen. Dad was already seated at the round wooden table and he looked up at them with mock gloom.

"I'm sorry to break the news, but the radio has already listed the Halcyon school as being closed today. A good thing. Our driveway is solid ice."

"What about our car?" Sandy asked.

Dad grimaced. "It's safely on ice. There'll be no towing it out until it stops snowing. I've phoned Mrs. Morris and she's going to open the store late today, so I don't need to go in this morning."

While they were eating breakfast the coating of snow on the ground thickened, and the evergreens began to show a powdering of white that made them more striking than ever. Sandy could see where the idea of snow on Christmas trees had come from. Only the real thing was more beautiful than any indoor imitation could be.

Mother went to phone Mrs. Haines and ask if Trina could stay a while longer, since there was no school. She came back to say that Trina's grandmother sounded a little calmer than before and she didn't seem to mind if Trina stayed longer.

"She's glad when I'm out of the house," said Trina dryly.

For an instant Sandy caught her mother's eye and they shared a moment of sadness. There might be good reason why Trina's grandmother didn't want her there.

As soon as they had finished breakfast, the two girls put on their outdoor things and went into the softly falling snow. Flakes were coming down thickly now and showed no sign of lessening, but Trina said it wasn't really a blizzard.

"When there's a blizzard the wind can blow so hard you can hardly stand up in it. Then the snow stings your face. And there are big drifts. Nobody likes to be outside in a blizzard."

Sandy remembered snowstorms in New York, but there it was different. In the city the snow was quickly dirty, because of people and cars. Out here in the country, a blizzard could isolate you from everyone else, just as the ice storm had done last night.

"Let's go out by the pond," Sandy said. "Then you can tell me more of what I'll need to know when I have to write my report for Mr. Wendel."

Outdoors, she found quickly that she had to be careful as she walked. Underneath the new snow everything was icy, and she slipped once or twice before she learned to put her feet down carefully without sliding them. In a little while the snow would become part of the ice surface, and the slipperiness would lessen. The big triangle of pond had iced over during the night, and snow had given it a smooth white surface.

In spite of falling snow, which had a tendency to muffle sound, the morning was anything but quiet. There were clattering sounds from the woods as ice fell from the trees, and sometimes whole branches broke off and crashed to the ground. Somewhere in the distance there was a sound of barking dogs, and Trina raised her head to listen.

"People ought to tie up their dogs when there's snow on the ground! The deer can't run as fast because they break through the surface, and the dogs get together in packs and hunt them."

Sandy shivered and tried to turn her mind to happier matters. At least the prickliness seemed to have gone out of Trina this morning and she was being almost friendly. It was as though she had begun to trust Sandy a little, and for some reason Sandy felt enormously pleased. To-day, at least, everything was going to be safe from un-pleasantness. Trina knew all sorts of things about the woods and the outdoors and the animals that Sandy found she was eager to learn. It was lovely to postpone Melissa and her friends—postpone the reckoning.

Or at least that was what she thought. The smashing of her hopes came more quickly than she expected.

Trina heard the sound of voices from the road and turned to look. Sandy looked in the same direction, and her spirits dropped several notches.

Down on Hemlock Road, plodding along in the snow, came Melissa Morris and Debra Elliot. Melissa's blue coat was bright against the whiteness, and Debra's brown was like the trees that lined their way—both powdered with snow. The two girls were talking and laughing together as they followed the road.

Beside Sandy, Trina had gone as still and as alert as the doe they had seen last night. Sandy put a hand on her arm.

"Wait," she said. "They may go right on by."

They did not go by. When they reached the foot of the Forster driveway, they stood for a moment looking toward the house. Then they started up the hill. They had not seen Trina and Sandy over by the pond.

9

Death in the Woods

"I'm going up in the woods," Trina said, her voice sounding rough again.

Sandy tightened her grip on Trina's arm. She dreaded whatever was coming, and she didn't want Trina to run away and leave her to face this alone.

"You can't go off and leave me," she cried. "You've got to help me if Melissa comes up here."

Trina gave her a slow, rather curious look. "What for? You don't have to stay here either. You can come up in the woods with me. I know places where they'll never find us. You don't have to be scared of those two."

The other girls were halfway up the drive, and still they had not seen Trina and Sandy by the pond. Their attention was on the house as they climbed toward it.

"I'm not afraid of them," Sandy insisted, though she knew this was hardly true. When she thought of Melissa's punching and hitting yesterday, she felt a quiver in her stomach. She wasn't any good at fighting. She didn't want a fight.

Trina made her favorite snorting sound of anger and scorn. "I'm not afraid either. I just don't want to have anything to do with those two."

The girls were coming closer. Any moment now they would turn their heads toward the pond.

"What I said just now"—Sandy faltered—"it wasn't true. I am afraid. But what they've been doing is wrong, and we'd better stay and face them. But you've got to help me. Only don't start hitting anybody or you'll make everything worse."

The girl beside her did not answer, but neither did she run off into the woods. After a moment Sandy took her hand from Trina's arm, knowing she would stay.

Melissa saw them first. She poked Debra and stood still on the drive, staring in their direction. Debra gave a little squeal when she saw them, and she stood still too. The snow came down as thickly, as softly as a white curtain, separating two groups of statues. Then Melissa moved.

"Come along," she commanded her companion, and both girls left the drive and started across the snow-covered grass, walking directly toward the two who waited.

To her surprise, Sandy saw that Melissa was smiling brightly. But it was a smile intended for Sandy, not Trina. Her right eye wore a dark bruise, and the scratches on her cheek were a reminder of yesterday. She ignored Trina as she and Debra neared the edge of the bond. Debra looked more uncomfortable and uncertain than Melissa. Her two ponytails stuck out jauntily beneath her knitted green stocking cap, but she looked anything but jaunty.

"Hello, Sandra," Melissa called. "Mr. Wendel phoned Mother and said that since there was no school today, I ought to come up here and see what I could learn about the pond for the ecology project. Debra stayed all night at my house, so we decided to walk over here together."

Sandy swallowed hard, trying to recover from her first alarm. "That's fine," she said, sounding stiff to her own ears.

The two came down to the edge of the snow-covered ice, to stand beside Sandy. Though Melissa continued to ignore Trina, Debra glanced at her curiously.

"Maybe you can tell us something about how the pond was built," Melissa said to Sandy, behaving as though there had never been any trouble between them.

This was some sort of game Melissa was playing, and Sandy did not trust her, but for the moment she would play along.

"It's Trina who knows all about how Mr. Seale had the pond built," she said. "You'd better ask her."

All she'd intended was to draw Trina into the conversation and get the other girls to accept her, perhaps to get Trina to talk as she had last night. She did not expect the sudden change in Trina.

"Sure," Trina said, without waiting for Melissa to ask any questions. "I can tell you about the pond. I was around most of the time while it was being built last summer. Mr. Seale thought this was a good level spot to dig, so he got a bulldozer in, and they piled up the dirt they dug out, and—"

Suddenly Sandy remembered Trina's promise last night to get even with Melissa and her friends, remembered her boast that she knew a way. This was the way. Nothing that came out of Trina's mouth was going to be true. And this would make everything worse. They ought to be working together as a committee, but Trina was separating them. Sandy took a deep breath and plunged into the middle of Trina's words.

Hurriedly, she told about the man from the U.S. Conservation Service coming in, and how men from the department had tested the ground and chosen the place where the pond would be built. When Trina tried to interrupt, she simply raised her voice and went right on, blurting out everything Trina had told about last night. All the things she could remember that were true. Melissa and Debra listened in astonishment, until she found she was out of information and ran down like a clock.

"Well!" Melissa said. "I didn't think you'd know all that."

Trina looked as though she was fighting with herself. When she finally spoke, it was with a rush of words.

"She doesn't! She got a lot of it wrong. Come on over here and you can see the place where a stream trickles down the hill. The spring that feeds it is just a little way up—where those stones are piled to direct it into the pond."

She led the way and the other three followed, Sandy feeling nervous again. But Trina seemed to have given up her original intent to mislead Melissa and tell her lies, and Sandy began to smile to herself. She knew what had happened. She *had* made mistakes, and Trina, who had been willing to give out the wrong information herself, suddenly couldn't endure the fact that she was being misquoted by someone else. Though Trina hardly talked at all in school, Sandy knew that she could talk well enough when she wanted to, and now she was full of her subject. Even Melissa stopped sneering, and Debra asked several good questions as they followed Trina around the end of the pond and onto the high grassy bank of the dam. The snow was deeper here, but at least it wasn't slippery.

Trina was talking about ground water now—about how rain and melting snow seeped deep into the earth, forming an underground source for the wells people had to dig in this area.

"Trees and plants help," Trina said. "They drink a lot of water, but they help hold it in the ground too, and keep it from running away to cause floods and erosion of good earth. That's the trouble with too many highways—the water runs off the concrete into ditches, and it's wasted or evaporates. Up here in the woods it sinks deep into the ground, and it's there when we need it. In dry spells there's only the deep ground water to feed our wells and springs. The water in ponds helps. Out in desert areas there's nothing to hold the surface water, and what is in the ground is too deep to be of any use—if it's there at all. Ponds preserve water and let it seep into the earth slowly. Look—over there is the overflow."

Sandy realized that Trina was using what must have been Mr. Seale's very words, echoing the things she had learned so well from him. All this was what she really knew.

As Trina walked on along the top of the dam she came to a sudden stop before something red that protruded from the snow. Her shoulders and knitted tam were white with flakes as she bent to pick up a long, winged object with a steel tip.

"Look at that!" she cried angrily, waving the arrow at them. "Here's what some bow-and-arrow hunter has shot up here on the dam. This property is all posted with warnings, but they've been here anyway, shooting at deer. The deer like to walk out on the dam, and they come down to the pond for water when it's not frozen. So they make real good targets."

The girls stood staring at the arrow in Trina's hands, and once more Sandy shivered. It seemed dreadful that anyone would want to shoot those beautiful, gentle deer.

Trina expressed her own thought. "It's not even sporting. The deer around here are so used to being safe that they just stand still and let a hunter shoot at them. The worst of it is, the hunter often misses and only wounds a deer. Then it runs away, wounded by shot. Or maybe with an arrow sticking into it. And it dies painfully unless the game warden can find it and kill it. Every year a lot of deer die slowly from wounds made by careless shooting."

"Oh, well," Melissa said, "the bow-and-arrow season only lasts a week, and it's over now. So whoever shot that arrow wasn't here today. Hunting with guns isn't as bad. My father used to go out early every morning during the hunting season, and sometimes he got a deer. Lots of men around here do. Sometimes they just hang a sign on their shop doors to say they've gone hunting, and nobody gets much else done that week. After all, if you don't thin out the deer by hunting them, the herds get too big, and they die of starvation in the wintertime when there isn't enough food for all."

Just the same, Sandy thought, *she* wouldn't want to kill any of these wild things, and she didn't think her father would either. Certainly Mr. Seale hadn't, since he'd posted his land so carefully.

Trina said nothing in answer to Melissa.

As they walked on along the dam, they came to where Mr. Seale had set up a tall pole with a large birdhouse on top of it—a white house with numerous apartments for bird families.

"That's a house for purple martins," Debra said. "They like to live near water, so they can use the mud for their nests and eat mosquitoes and other bugs that collect around ponds."

"Maybe that's what you could write about for Mr. Wendel," Sandy said. "Our papers have to add up to a whole picture." Debra blinked at her.

A little farther along, Trina showed them the place where a big concrete enclosure emerged above the frozen surface of the pond and explained that it was connected to a pipe that had been built into the dam. The other end came out far down the bank on the other side, where it could let the overflow run into a small stream that had once led directly from the spring on the uphill side.

"You can see that even though most of the pond is frozen, there's an overflow at this point," Trina said. "But what doesn't overflow will be held and preserved. Then, even when it's dry, you can get water for irrigation and fire protection. Besides that, all sorts of things live and grow in a pond. Plants and water creatures. So there will be food for the fish that Mr. Seale has stocked."

"Why don't the fish freeze in winter?" Sandy asked.

Trina threw her a superior look. "Because ponds don't freeze at the bottom. The fish are down there now, swimming around. In the spring you can see them, and they'll be frogs and all sorts of water bugs."

Debra was listening to all this knowledge in outright astonishment. Melissa did not look altogether pleased, but she wanted a good mark on the paper she meant to write, so she was listening too.

Sandy could see a problem arising if they all tried to write about the pond.

"Maybe the five of us—Ginger, too—could divide up the subjects connected with all this. There must be enough in what Trina's telling us to make up five different papers. Then we won't all be working against each other by writing the same things."

Melissa smiled sweetly. "That's a good idea, Sandra. But it won't do Trina any good. No matter how much she thinks she knows, she'll get a bad mark because she's no good at putting words down on paper. She spells everything wrong and she can't write proper sentences."

That, Sandy thought, was not fair. And she didn't think Mr. Wendel would mark only on good writing. What Trina knew had to count for something. But before she could answer Melissa, a voice hailed them from below the dam. Cliff Wendel was coming through the woods from the direction of the road. He wore a red lumber jacket and a green cap, layered with snow.

"Hey!" he called. "Have you seen any hunters?"

Trina held up the arrow. "We haven't seen any, but we found this."

"No—these are two men with guns. Dad saw them cutting up through the woods, so he sent me to let Mr. Forster know."

"Then let's go tell him," Sandy said, and they all hurried along the top of the dam and around the end of the pond in the direction of the house.

As they ran, a shot sounded from up on the mountain, then another. Inside the house, Mr. Forster heard the shots and came out on the porch just as the five ran across the snowy grass.

"A couple of hunters went up into your woods," Cliff said. "If you can get their numbers, you can turn them in to the warden. I'll go up with you, if you like."

"Thanks," Dad said. "I'll be out in a minute." He dashed inside and was back almost at once. He had already put his boots on and was pulling on his red cap and heavy short coat as he came out the door.

"Let's go," he said to Cliff, and the two set off up the trail.

Trina did not wait to be asked or told to stay behind. She simply ran after the two men. Melissa, Debra, and Sandy stared at each other for a moment, and then followed without a word. With Melissa's bright blue coat in their midst, no hunters were going to mistake them for deer, and they didn't want to miss whatever might happen. Nevertheless, they stayed a little behind the first group and moved through the snow noiselessly, lest Mr. Forster look around and tell them to go back. At least he had accepted Trina—perhaps because she knew the trails so well.

As they climbed the mountain, the crashing of falling ice was all around, and once or twice ice pellets showered them. By the time they reached the ridge where the ground dipped down to the cabin, they found the other three standing below, with something stretched on the ground before them. Sandy caught her breath in dismay. Neither Melissa nor Debra, who had both grown up in the country, seemed especially upset, but Sandy walked slowly behind them as they went down to join Mr. Forster and Cliff. In the end, however, she had to look at the pitiful object on the ground. There were no alert ears, no flag of a white tail. The eyes were no longer gentle and mildly curious but were wild with terror and pain, the whites showing around the dark centers. Blood stained the snow, and gray-brown fur was matted with blood. Even as they watched, the eyes grew glassy and the agony faded. The doe made a last weak effort to stand, and then life went out of her with a small rushing sigh as she breathed her last breath.

Sandy heard Cliff's echoing sigh. "It's a good thing. We haven't a gun along to stop her suffering."

Mr. Forster spoke angrily. "Those hunters aren't only breaking the law by coming onto this land, they're also breaking it by shooting a doe."

"Look!" Cliff said, pointing.

A trail of footprints led through the snow, up into the woods away from the path.

Mr. Forster started to follow them, with Cliff beside him, and then turned back to speak to Trina.

"Do you know how to get the game warden on the phone?"

"Sure," Trina said.

"Then go back to the house and call him. Tell him a doe has been killed up here. You girls go with her."

He waited for no answer, but went off into the woods at a jog, Cliff right behind him. Trina started down the trail at once, and after a brief hesitation, Melissa and Debra went with her. For a moment longer Sandy hung back miserably, her attention still upon the slain doe. Just a little while ago this creature had belonged to the woods. She had been alive and beautiful. Perhaps this was the very one that had stood looking in through candlelit windows during the blackout, with her two children feeding nearby. Now she was dead and the two fawns were without a mother. Ecology might be a subject in school—but this was life and death. This was breaking everything down into what really happened.

She walked along slowly in the wake of the others, too shocked and unhappy to want anyone's company. As she followed the trail, she stared at the tracks they were leaving along the path, both going and coming. It wasn't snowing as hard as before, and the tracks were still clear on the white ground. She could see that deer had come this way too, making deep hoof indentations as they broke through the snow. Sometimes she gazed into the woods around her. Black outcroppings of rock rose from the snowy ground, and tree trunks looked black against all the whiteness. Everything seemed beautiful—and terrible.

Once, beside the path, she came to a tree that had apparently been clawed by some large animal. There were long scratches down the trunk, and pieces of bark lay on the ground at the foot of the tree. She told herself she would ask Trina about this. She wanted to know everything about the wildlife of the forest, and about the trees that grew here. Perhaps her subject would be the animals themselves. Trina could tell her about them, and Mother had an animal book at the house. In return, perhaps she could help Trina write her paper. She would ask Mr. Wendel if that could be allowed.

Yet all this seemed aside from what she had just seen in the death of the doe. Not until the two parts began to come together would she know and understand these things as Trina did. Mr. Wendel and Cliff had talked in terms of her helping Trina. But it wasn't going to be like that. Trina had a special value in herself. It might be that it was Trina who would do the most for Sandy Forster.

She began to feel a little better as she walked along. Now, at least, she did not need to dread going back to school as much as she had.

Before she reached the house shots sounded again on the mountain, and she stood still on the path and gazed about her at the peaceful, snowy woods. The crackle of sound that echoed along the mountain and was flung back at her from piles of rock was somehow terrifying because she did not know what it meant. She had the horrible fear that the hunters might have turned and fired at their human pursuers. This fear was not helped by what Melissa said when Sandy got back to the house.

Trina had gone inside to telephone the game warden, and the other two were waiting on the porch. They had heard the shots, and were staring up into the woods, though the rise of the mountain was steep behind the house and they could not see beyond it.

"It's usually hunters who come in from somewhere else that cause trouble," Melissa said. "Local people have more respect for their neighbors' posting. But that makes it all the worse because strangers can drive off without ever being seen again. Unless your father and Cliff can get a good look at the numbers the hunters have to wear on their backs if they have a license, there isn't much chance of catching them."

Sandy did not want to talk about hunting and killing. She wanted to quiet the fright that was making her heart thump so roughly in her chest.

"I'll bet you were surprised at how much Trina could tell us about the pond," she said, trying to change the subject.

Debra nodded agreement. "I'd never have thought—" she began, but Melissa broke in on her words.

"Of course she'd know all that. She watched the pond being built last summer. And she practically lives out in the woods. Anyway, we can let her help us for a while."

Sandy could see what Melissa meant. She would take Trina's help as long as it was useful. And Sandy Forster could help too, by letting Melissa and the others come over to study the pond at firsthand. But what about afterward?

The look in Melissa's eyes told her the truth. Nothing had been forgiven or forgotten. Afterward, Melissa would line the other girls up against Trina, and probably against Sandy too. They would follow Melissa's lead and everything would be right back at its worst. There didn't seem to be a thing in the world Sandy Foster could do about it.

In the beginning Trina hadn't wanted to talk to Melissa,

or to help her, but Sandy had fixed it so that Trina would want to tell what she really knew. And Melissa had used her. Sandy walked down the steps—away from Melissa and Debra. It wasn't fair that Trina should be taken advantage of, when, for once, she had done the right thing.

Behind her, Melissa said, "Come on, Debra—let's start home. We've got enough information about the pond to write up our papers."

Sandy whirled about. "We didn't decide which of us would write about what. I think Trina ought to do the pond. And I'd like to write about the animals that live in the woods."

Melissa shrugged. "That's your idea. We don't have to write about different things. I'm going home and write my paper now, so I can turn it in tomorrow. Come on, Debra."

This wasn't the way a committee should work, and Debra hesitated for a moment, as though she might be considering an argument with Melissa.

Sandy spoke quickly. "You don't have to go now, Debra, unless you want to."

For a moment longer Debra hesitated. Melissa was already stamping down the snowy drive. Then Debra shrugged helplessly and plodded after her. When Melissa saw she was coming, she stopped and waited for her with a bright, rewarding smile.

As they went down the hill, Trina came out of the house. She seemed more alive and interested than Sandy had ever seen her.

"I talked to Mr. Murtagh, the game warden," she said, "and he's coming right over to take the dead deer away. He'll want to talk to your father to see if he can find out anything about the hunters who killed it." She glanced toward the road and saw Melissa and Debra trudging along. "Are they going home?"

Sandy nodded. "Melissa says she's going to write about the building of the pond. I told her that was for you to write about."

"She'll do as she pleases. Anyway, she can put the words down right, and I can't. So what does it matter?"

"I'll help you," Sandy said quickly. "I'm pretty good at writing assignments, and I don't think Mr. Wendel will mind. After all—look how you've helped me."

"I don't want anybody's help!" The dark look had

descended upon Trina again like a lowering storm cloud. She started past Sandy toward the pond.

Sandy ran after her. Asking for Trina's help had served once before—she would try it again.

"But I need you! I want to write about the animals in the woods, and I have such a lot to learn. There's so much you can tell me. Mr. Wendel says ecology is about all living things and their surroundings, so wild animals fit in."

Trina seemed not to hear her. She reached the edge of the pond on the opposite shore from the dam and stood looking at the scene before her.

"Won't you help me?" Sandy asked.

"Why should I? I helped Melissa, didn't I? I didn't want to, but I did. And you can see how she's acting. She'll put down everything I told her, and Mr. Wendel will think she's wonderful."

"Mr. Wendel will know where she got her information."

"But he'll give her a good mark anyway."

Sandy could think of no answer, no solution. She stood beside Trina, staring out across the snow-covered film of ice, while thick flakes drifted down from the sky. The wind had begun to blow, and it was growing colder, snowing harder. She felt helpless and defeated—and thoroughly bewildered.

The girl beside her spoke softly, unexpectedly. "You should see what all this will be like when it's spring."

Sandy threw her a quick look. Trina's personal storm clouds seemed to have lifted because of some vision in her mind.

"There'll be grasses growing green all around the banks. We'll see the fish again, and hear the frogs when they plop into the water. All the pond will come alive. Along the roads wild flowers will be coming up. Mustard and columbine and blue flag. Blue flag is wild iris, you know."

"I don't know anything about wild flowers," Sandy admitted. "Except maybe daisies and buttercups. And dandelions."

"There'll be those too. And later on wild carrot—that's Queen Anne's lace. Farmers don't like it because if cows eat it, their milk tastes strong, the way the plant smells when you crush it. But I think it's the most beautiful wild flower of all—just like white lace. Once I picked a bouquet of it for my grandmother and fixed it in a vase on the table near my mother's picture."

"Was she pleased?"

"Her! She had a fit. She took it and threw it all out the back door. Because she said you don't put weeds in flower vases." Trina sounded angry again. "She only likes neat flower beds and things that grow in pots. She doesn't care anything about the flowers that grow wild in fields and woods."

"Then she must be missing a lot," Sandy said. Trina was glowering now, and she wished she could please her, cheer her up.

Snow had already filled in their earlier tracks around the pond, but Trina had given her a picture of how it would be with snow and winter gone and flowers coming up everywhere, birds returning from the south, the animals that had slept all winter emerging to a new spring world, and the pond waking to life in its own mysterious way.

Marks in the snow at her feet seemed suddenly more significant than ever, because they meant that some live thing had come this way. It was not only information—it was this feeling she wanted to get into her report. A feeling that was a newborn part of herself, instead of being mere facts she got from somewhere else.

"What are those?" she asked, pointing.

"Rabbit tracks," Trina said shortly.

Sandy studied the marks in the snow. "Perhaps I could draw a sketch of rabbit tracks," she mused. "And other tracks too, if I can find them. I could make small pictures and use them when I write about the animals. That is, I could, if you'd help me."

Trina gave her a long, cool look. "Why should I?" she repeated. "And why should you care anyway—about getting good marks, I mean?"

"It's not the marks! It's something important I want to do. I know only about the city. Now I want to learn about the country. It's fun to learn about all these things."

"Fun!" Trina echoed. "What a sucker you are!"

Sandy was suddenly impatient. She turned so she could look directly into Trina's green eyes which seemed to shine in the snow light.

"I'd think you were stupid if I didn't know better!" she cried. "Here you are, practically an expert in all sorts of ways. You thought Mr. Seale was wonderful, and you could probably grow up to be like him. You heard Mr. Wendel say in class that there are all kinds of jobs opening up in ecology these days. You'd have it easier than most of us because you already know what you could do, and you're learning about it now. But if you act in school as if you were stupid, and if you don't learn how to put words on paper, and spell properly, and if you don't like to read—you'll cut yourself off from everything that's good and useful and interesting. And that's stupid!"

Trina blinked at her in surprise, as though a rabbit had turned and bitten her. But before she could answer, Dad's voice hailed them from the woods as he and Cliff came out upon the snowy lawn. Sandy ran toward them, while Trina hung back.

"Did you catch the hunters? Did you get their numbers?"

Dad shook his head. "We followed their tracks. They were shooting again, and we tried to catch up with them, but they heard us coming and crashed off through the woods and down to a car they had parked on the highway. We saw them drive off, but we were too far away to get the number on their jackets, or on the license plate. Did Trina call the game warden?"

"She called him," Sandy said, "and he's coming over as soon as he can." She turned back toward Trina, but the other girl had left the bank of the pond and was already on her way down the drive without saying good-by, or uttering a word of thanks for staying overnight at the Forsters'. Her back seemed to announce that she had no further interest in the slain deer, or anything else that concerned Sandy Forster.

Sandy watched her plod down to the road. Trina had simply decided to shut everyone out again and was going off by herself. It looked as though her morning of knowing more than anybody else had done nothing at all to make her feel better.

Dad thanked Cliff for helping him, and went up on the porch, beating snow from his shoulders and arms, stamping it from his boots. Sandy followed him into the house, and as soon as she had taken off her outdoor things, she went looking for her mother.

She found her sitting on the living room couch with a nature book open on her knees. Sandy sat down beside her and began to talk out all her worry about Melissa and her friends on the one hand, and Trina on the other. Mother listened thoughtfully, putting in a question or a comment now and then. When Sandy fell silent, she reached an arm about her daughter's shoulders.

"This is a real and serious problem," she said, "and I'm glad you want to do something about it. But right now you need more help than I can give you. Why don't you go down and talk to Mr. Wendel?"

Sandy started to shake her head in dismay, but Mother went on quickly.

"I know you feel you aren't very well acquainted with him yet, but I think you'll find him easy to talk to. He knows these girls and the whole situation better than we do, and I think talking to him may help. So will you?"

Sandy didn't really want to consult Mr. Wendel, but something had to be done. After a moment she nodded.

"Good!" Mother said. "Wait here and I'll phone and see if you can go and talk to him now."

She gave Sandy no chance for further doubts, but hurried off to the telephone.

Perhaps this was the best way after all—even though it might be hard to talk to a teacher she had known only for a few days. Anyway, she would try.

10

A Matter of Sharing

A fire burned brightly in the big stone fireplace in the Wendel living room. Cliff knelt before the hearth popping corn and piling the white kernels in a big green bowl. Outside the nearest window, gray-and-white juncos—snow birds—were taking turns at sunflower seeds and suet, along with chickadees, downy woodpeckers, and a tufted titmouse. There was even a pair of red cardinals which came in autocratically, chasing the other birds away.

Cliff knew the names of all the birds and he told Sandy about them as they flew in and out of the bird feeder, sometimes pecking at each other as well as at the seeds. There were bullies among birds too.

Mr. Wendel sat in a big armchair and waited for what Sandy had to say. She found it hard to begin. He knew a little of it—about the way Melissa and the others had teased Trina, and how Trina had struck back. But he knew nothing of the things that had happened this morning, and she found it hard to tell him. Trina had meant to give Melissa the wrong information, so she would get a bad mark on her paper. But because of Sandy's efforts, Trina had wound up giving the right information after all. This much she could tell. But her feeling that Melissa meant to use this and then behave toward Trina just as she had before was not something she could explain. Anyway, she hadn't come to Mr. Wendel to make accusations.

"I thought we might divide up the subjects," she said hesitantly. "I mean, Trina could write about the pond and water, and maybe I could choose the animals. And the others could take birds and trees and plants, and even the earth. There are lots of subjects."

"A very good idea," Mr. Wendel said. "It might help still more if you each try to see how your own subject is tied into all the others. Of course this will make it a bigger project and will take more time than we'd planned. But it could be worth it."

"Except that Trina would have to help us," Sandy said. "And I don't think she will. She's already mad at Melissa, and she's peeved with me because I got her to talk to us this morning. Melissa told her she wouldn't get a good mark anyway, because Trina isn't good at writing things out." Sandy hesitated, and then went on, faltering. "Perhaps—perhaps I could help her on that—if she'd let me."

A log in the grate fell with a shower of sparks and burned into a red ember. Cliff was through with the corn popper, and the bowl beside him was piled high with white puffs of corn. But Cliff made no effort to pass the bowl around.

After a thoughtful moment Mr. Wendel asked a question. "Do you like Trina, Sandy?"

It was Sandy's turn to be thoughtful. That was a hard question to answer.

"At first I didn't like her," she admitted. "Then—well—I began to find out what she was like when she wasn't being rough and mean. But I don't know whether I really like her or not. I wanted to have a friend. But I don't know if Trina will ever be anybody's friend. She could if she wanted to. But I don't know if she'll ever want to."

"You worry about her, don't you?"

"Worry about her?"

"Isn't it because you're worried that you've come to talk to me? So that we can figure out some way of helping her?"

Sandy seemed to keep repeating his words. *"Helping* her?" She stared into the fire for a moment. How could she make Mr. Wendel understand something she didn't altogether understand herself?

"You don't like that word?" he asked gently.

She shook her head, unable to explain.

"Perhaps you've got something there. Perhaps when we think of helping others we sometimes put ourselves in a superior position—even when we don't mean to. We don't seem altogether fair or truly generous."

"Yes," Sandy said. "I think that's it. Because Trina was helping me too."

"Perhaps there's a better word. A word that can bring people together on equal terms. We might call it sharing."

Sharing—Sandy sounded it over in her mind. "I like that better. But"—she was still groping—"I don't want to share anything with Melissa. I don't like Melissa Morris!"

Mr. Wendel smiled at her emphasis. "We're not required to like everyone. It's pretty human not to. But we try not to injure the ones we don't like. Perhaps we even try to understand them."

Sandy nodded. He made her feel a little better about everything. But there was still no real answer. She stared into the fire for a while and Cliff smiled at her—as though he approved of her now. Not at all the way he'd looked yesterday in the school yard. When she glanced at Mr. Wendel again she found he was watching her with kind, understanding eyes.

"You'll do all right, Sandy," he said. "You're not one of those we have to worry about. Because you know how to share."

"Share what?" Sandy was still puzzled. "What have I got to share?"

"Yourself, mainly. You get involved. You're already sharing yourself with Trina when you come here to try to help her. It's healthy to be able to share. Trina doesn't know how. Perhaps Melissa doesn't either."

"But why does Trina behave the way she does? Why does she do everything in the worst possible way, so that she only hurts herself?"

"The answer to that probably dips into the subject of psychology," Mr. Wendel said. "But you're old enough to understand about human motivation—that is, what prompts human beings to act the way they do. What do *you* want most in life? What do *you* think are the necessary things to make you a happy, useful human being? Because, of course, when we're useful we're happy."

That was hard to answer right off, but she tried to think about it. "I suppose just now I want a friend. I don't want to be alone."

"Right," Mr. Wendel said. "That comes under the heading of love. We find love with our family and our friends."

She stared at him, suddenly understanding. "And Trina doesn't have much of that."

"Exactly. And you do have it—with your mother and father and your friends."

"I haven't any friends here," Sandy said.

"But you will have—before you know it."

"Not if I side with Trina. Not if Melissa turns everyone against me."

"Give yourself time. Melissa doesn't run the school. I'm

sorry she's giving you such a poor opinion of Halcyon. People aren't really like that around here. It's unfortunate that the troublemakers are often the ones who get noticed most easily. You'll find other girls in our room whom you'll like. You don't know them yet, and they don't know you. It takes a little while. Something will happen to turn the tide—you'll see. You're doing the right things to make yourself a friend. Trina isn't. But that's only one part of life. What else do you want?"

"I don't know . . . maybe to be part of what's happening."

"Right again. That's what we call contributing. Everyone wants other people to recognize and approve of what he's doing. What about Trina there?"

"Zero," Sandy said. "She doesn't want to be a part of anything."

"Don't be too sure about that. It's human to want to be noticed and recognized. Unfortunately, she's found she can get recognition by causing trouble, by doing wild things, and getting attention in all the wrong ways."

"But that's not a good choice for her to make!"

"Of course it isn't. She's off down a foolish road, running with all her might in the wrong direction. Something needs to trip her up, turn her around, make her understand what she's doing. Perhaps this morning when she helped you with information about the pond she got a taste of a different way to get attention—a more satisfying way. The fault in choosing the wrong way is that it continues to be unsatisfying."

"I don't think it's made any difference," Sandy said. "She's just as mad as ever at everybody."

"We can't know that for sure. She's had a sampling of something better, and she may come back for more. Sometimes a change that seems to come suddenly may really result from a slow growth that has been going on underneath."

"But Trina's grandmother doesn't like her, and—"

"I know. And I'm afraid Mrs. Haines will be very hard to change. In any situation, there may be some things we can do nothing about. But if outside matters improve, Trina may find more strength to deal sensibly with what's difficult at home. Some of her trouble there is of her own making, as you've probably seen. But this is why your interest in Trina is important. You may be the outside influence that helps her."

Once more, Sandy had an immediate and disturbing reaction to this suggestion, just as she'd had when Cliff had said much the same thing.

"No—no, I don't want to! Trina gets me into trouble. She doesn't even like me. And she says she won't help me on the ecology project."

For the first time Cliff broke in. "You can't always believe what people say when they're upset, Sandy. We all get mad and say things we don't mean when we think about them later."

Restlessly, Sandy got to her feet. She bent toward the fire and warmed hands that suddenly felt cold. She hated the way she was being pushed toward Trina.

Mr. Wendel seemed to understand a little of what she felt. "You have to choose your own way, Sandy. We all have to do that in the long run. Choices can be given us, but *we* have to choose. With Trina, it's partly that she hasn't been given the right choices."

"Melissa said that no matter how much Trina knows, she'll get a low mark on her paper because she isn't good at writing. Is that so?"

Mr. Wendel got up and stood beside her looking into the fire. He wasn't very tall. In a few years Cliff would be taller than his father. But Sandy knew now how impressive he could be because of what went on inside him. She had the feeling that he was a truly good person.

When he spoke, his words were grave. "I don't teach that way, Sandy. I don't believe in failures in my classroom. I believe in growing, in helping people to grow. We can all do better today than we did yesterday, and in progress there isn't any failure. If you can help Trina with what she needs to put on paper, she'll learn from the experience. And if she helps you, that's sharing. That's growing. Perhaps she may even learn that there's a use for being able to read and write well. A use that's important to her and will bring her a lot of satisfaction. Next time she'll do a little better—and that's what counts. So go ahead and help her."

Sandy's sigh was deep and discouraged. "She said she didn't want me to help her."

"Words!" Cliff put in again. "Just words. Don't pay any attention." He reached for the green bowl. "Won't you like some popcorn? And you just go right on helping her, anyway."

Munching on popcorn made a welcome relief from talk that was becoming too difficult. Popcorn gave her an escape from words. When Sandy had eaten a handful or two, she said she must go home, and she thanked Mr. Wendel for talking to her. She wasn't in the least sure that the talking had helped, but she knew he had tried and hadn't brushed her worries aside.

Mr. Wendel walked to the door with her when she left. "You've given me a good idea, Sandy. You know that log cabin Mr. Seale built up in the woods?"

Sandy nodded.

"Would your father mind if you used it as a sort of clubhouse after school for a few days?"

"He wouldn't mind. But I don't know what you mean."

"I'm going to announce in class tomorrow that more will be accomplished if these various ecology committees break up the subjects, so that each person in a group takes a different phase of ecology but tries to tie it into the subjects the others are studying. We'll put off the time when the papers need to be in. Then I'll suggest privately that the members of your committee start meeting up in the woods in your cabin and work out together what subject each of you will take. That will put Trina right on the ground where she's at home and knows a great deal. What do you think of that?"

"She'll have a fit," Sandy said. "She acts as though that cabin belongs to her. She even hates to have me go into it."

"All the more reason for her to learn to share it," Mr. Wendel said. "I'll make the suggestion, and then you do the best you can to smooth things out and get it to work. Will you try, Sandy?"

She had no answer for him. There was no promise she could make with confidence.

A few moments later she was walking along the road through deepening snow. Walking had grown more difficult because with each step on the soft surface she sank in. But she did not think about the difficult walking because she was turning over in her mind some of the things Mr. Wendel had said. For instance, his words about sharing. Her cheeks grew warm with pleasure, even out here in the

cold, when she recalled what he had said about her getting
along well because she knew how to share.

But hadn't Trina moved a little in that direction once or
twice in the last few days? She remembered that moment
yesterday after Trina had roughed up Melissa and then
run away—and Sandy had found her in the cabin. Trina
had taken the things out of her treasure box and shown
them to Sandy, one by one. Hadn't that been a kind of
sharing, even though she'd changed later? Trina had
shared her knowledge with all of them too, though perhaps
that was only because she wanted to show off a little and
correct the mistakes Sandy was making.

There was still another time. There was the moment just
a little while ago when Trina had stood looking at the
pond, sharing with Sandy a picture of what it would be
like when spring came. Trina had moved in Sandy's direction then, and had given her something that was Trina's
own. At those times she had liked Trina.

Nevertheless, Trina never stayed likable, and that was
the trouble.

Before Sandy reached home the worries had crowded
back, and her fears of what Melissa could do, her concern
about the difficult road down which Trina could so easily
take her.

That afternoon, as the snowstorm blew itself into a real
blizzard, Sandy took refuge in a book and read for a long
while, letting her own troubles go as she followed those of
a girl in a story who had even worse problems than her
own. When she put the book aside, she felt a little better.

After that, she spent some time looking at pictures of
animal tracks in Dad's encyclopedia. She wanted to be
able to recognize them when she saw them outside in the
snow. Perhaps she wouldn't even need Trina. But she
could not quite put away from herself the fact that Trina
and she needed each other—whether Trina accepted that
or not.

11

Blood on the Snow

The storm was short-lived, after all. Late in the afternoon the snow lessened and ceased to fall. The gusty wind died down, the sun broke through gray clouds and the county began to dig itself out. Snowplows and sanders were out on the highway, and the county plow came along Hemlock Road. Dad even managed to get his car pulled out of the ditch. That night Sandy went to bed knowing there would be school tomorrow and beginning to dread it all over again.

During the interval she saw nothing more of Trina or of the other girls, but her thoughts were never far away from them.

In the morning Dad drove Sandy and her mother in to school, since Mrs. Venner had asked to see them. Melissa and her mother, and Mrs. Haines and Trina, were already in the principal's office, and the whole unhappy incident had to be gone over again. It was not a pleasant interview, and Mrs. Morris was inclined to blame Sandy and Trina, while Trina's grandmother obviously agreed with anyone who blamed her granddaughter—and for Trina that made everything that much worse.

Sandy's mother took a moderate view of what had happened, and made Mrs. Venner understand about the teasing that had led to the explosion, something Mrs. Morris had not been told about. When the three girls went to their classroom, Sandy had the feeling that everything had been stirred up again. But at least there would be no more teasing of Trina on school grounds.

When they joined the class in progress, Mr. Wendel lost no time in suggesting his change of plans and explaining it in detail. Melissa wailed that it wasn't fair—she had already written her paper. She had written about the pond on the Forster property, and she didn't want to do it all over.

"Then perhaps you'll want to talk this over with the other members of your committee," Mr. Wendel said.

"That's pretty fast work, and there may be quite a bit more you'll want to add when you've discussed it with the others."

He said nothing about the cabin, but true to his promise, when recess came, he stopped the girls of Melissa's committee and gathered them around his desk.

"Sandy has been good enough to offer the use of her father's cabin up in the woods," he told them. "So you'll have the advantage of your own meeting place where you can decide how you're going to work, and what subjects you'll each choose. The cabin will be a center for you to work from, right there in the woods. Since you'll have the advantage of the forest to work in, I suggest that your topics concern that area. You can leave the subjects of air and water pollution to one of the other committees."

Sandy glanced quickly at Trina, and saw that she was staring out of a window, looking sullen and uninterested, as if she had removed herself entirely from the group. Her mouth was set in a stubborn line, and Sandy guessed that the session in Mrs. Venner's office and the things Mrs. Haines had said were still rankling. Trina was undoubtedly mad about anyone's using the cabin.

Melissa had a question. "Won't some of the other kids in our room be working on the same subjects we'll be studying and reporting on?"

"That won't matter," Mr. Wendel said. "You won't be working together, and it will be interesting to see what different—or similar—facts you come up with. I suggest that you get started today, right after school."

He paused and looked at Trina, who was still staring out of the window.

"I'd also like to suggest," he went on, "that Trina Carpozi be put in charge of your group—each committee needs a chairman. I don't think any of you know as much about these things as she does, and it will be valuable to you to have her as your guide. Will that be all right with you, Trina?"

Trina brought her thoughts back to the room with difficulty. She had heard him, but clearly she did not like what she had heard. He was waiting for an answer, however, and the other girls were looking at her. Under her breath, Sandy found herself pleading silently, *Be nice, Trina! Be nice!*

But Trina only looked around with her usual glowering

air. "I'm going to do the pond," she said flatly. "I know more about it than I told yesterday. I know more about it than Melissa does."

"But I've got it done and you haven't," Melissa said sharply.

Mr. Wendel refused to get into this argument. "You'll have to take that up among yourselves. What I'm interested in now, Trina, is whether you're willing to take on the leadership of the group. How do you feel about that?"

It was easy to see, Sandy thought, that a struggle was going on inside Trina. All her instincts and all her past behavior made her want to fling the entire project back at the other girls, refuse to help them, refuse to have anything to do with it. If she had been able to, she would probably have forbidden them to use the cabin. But there was a new and contrary struggle going on in her at the same time, and you could almost see the uncertainties of that struggle in her face. Probably no one had ever asked Trina to take charge of anything before, and in spite of herself some sort of pride was rising in her. But Trina had practiced being unpleasant for too long to give up her old ways, and you could almost see the wrong side winning out.

"They don't need any leader," she said crossly. "I'm not going to tell them all a lot of stuff so they can go away and use it without doing any work."

"I'm sorry you feel that way," Mr. Wendel said, "because I'm afraid that whether you like it or not, these girls must look to you to share your knowledge with them. I hope you'll give it. They need you, Trina."

Trina shrugged sullenly, without answering—and that was the end of the discussion.

Mr. Wendel dismissed them, and Melissa, Debra, and Ginger all hurried from the room. Trina followed, but far enough behind so they would not speak to her. Sandy lingered in the room with Mr. Wendel.

He shook his head at her ruefully. In a way, they were partners in this attempt. "It didn't work, did it?"

"Maybe not," Sandy said, "but for a second or two I think Trina really wanted to do what you were asking her."

"Which is a step in the right direction," Mr. Wendel admitted. "As a matter of fact, I didn't expect her to go along with my suggestion immediately, and it might not have worked if she had. Because I doubt that Melissa and her friends are ready to accept Trina as a leader. Not yet. We'll see what happens when the pressure is on and they need to find out what they don't know."

Sandy smiled, liking him. "I'll tell you what happens," she promised.

At least there was no more teasing of Trina for the rest of that day. Melissa's games had been discarded, and Trina kept her distance warily. Not even Sandy could get near her. She simply walked away when she saw one of them coming, as though she wanted to prove that she needed none of them in her life, and was certainly not going to hand out any more free information as she had done yesterday. During classes she was her usual lumpish self, showing no interest in anything. Sandy found herself marveling that this was the same girl who had shown her a vision of spring yesterday.

At noon Sandy took her lunch box, and got permission to go down the road to the Morris Hardware Store. Her father was in the back of the store eating his own lunch which Mother had packed for him that morning. Later on, he'd said, he might drive home for lunch, but for now he would stay close to the store and spell Mrs. Morris when she went home at noon. He greeted Sandy with pleasure.

"Hi, there! This is a good surprise. Here, I'll fix a place for you to sit."

He lifted a cardboard carton off a rickety chair and dusted it with a none-too-clean cloth. Sandy sat down and opened her lunch box.

"Trade you," she said.

They happily traded pickles for peanuts and ham for cheese. It wasn't that they didn't like their own lunches, but what turned up in someone else's box always seemed more interesting. And Mother never packed duplicates.

"Now then," Dad said when they were chewing contentedly, "don't tell me, let me guess. I am honored by your company because you have a problem."

"Mm," said Sandy around a mouthful of ham. "Trina's my problem."

Dad sighed. "Not again. Is she stirring up more trouble at school?"

"She wasn't the one who started all the trouble," Sandy protested.

"No, but she certainly increased it. What's up now?"

"The ecology committee I'm on is coming to our place after school today. We'd like to go up to the cabin in the woods. Mr. Wendel thought it would make a good clubhouse for us. We're going to decide on the subjects each of us will study. I think I'm going to do wild animals. I mean whatever kind of animals live in the woods. I'm supposed to find out how they help the land and the forest, and other animals, and even people."

"Very in-ter-est-ing," Dad said, sounding like television. "That will take a good forty years' work. I congratulate you."

"Don't be silly. Of course I can't learn it all in a hurry, but I can collect enough to write a good report for Mr. Wendel. He's been trying to get Trina to help us, but I'm not sure she will. He wanted her to be the leader, but I guess that's out."

Dad seemed a little bemused by the thought of Trina as a leader, though he said nothing.

"So will it be all right if we use the cabin?" Sandy asked.

"Of course. Though with all the snow that fell yesterday, its' not going to be easy—slogging up through the woods. You'd need snowshoes. Tell you what I'll do. I'll take an hour or two off this afternoon and pick you girls up at school in my car. Then I'll take you home and get out the snowmobile Mr. Seale sold me. I can give you a lift, two at a time, up to the cabin. The snowmobile will pack down the trail, so you won't have as much trouble walking back to the house when you're through with your meeting."

Sandy grinned at him. "That's wonderful! There's five of us on the committee, so be sure you take Trina and me up together. Then she won't have to ride alone."

"Right," he said and gave her a little cuff of approval on her cheek.

When she'd finished lunch she went back to school and sought out Melissa. As usual, Debra and Ginger were with her. She told them about the arrangements Dad had suggested and asked them to wait with her after school. Then she went looking for Trina.

She found her sitting on a low stone wall on the far side of the school building, staring off into space. When Sandy had told her the plans she spoke without turning her head.

"I'm not going," she said in her usual blunt way.

Sandy had half expected this and she had already thought about how to meet it. She put on her most dramatic expression of dismay, trying to look as though utter calamity had descended upon her.

"But I can't do the animals by myself!" she wailed. "I have to ask you about tracks, and what animals there are up in the woods, and how they live, and all that. How do I know any of this?"

"You can read it in books," Trina said gruffly. "Do your own work for a change."

Sandy stifled a temptation to retort angrily. Trina was the worst possible person for rubbing one the wrong way.

"Look," she said, with still more pleading in her voice, "I'm new here in Halcyon. And I've already been in trouble. I want to make up for that and turn in some good work. I'd like Mr. Wendel to be pleased with me. But I can't do it without you."

For a moment Trina looked as if she might waver. "Well, maybe I'll help you. But not the others. And I won't come up there while they're in the cabin."

Sandy stopped being dramatically desperate and tried another approach. Somehow Trina must be coaxed into working with all the girls. Helping just one wasn't enough.

"Do you want them to go up to the cabin and open drawers and find the box you keep up there?"

Trina's look darkened. "They'd better not!"

"Then you'll need to be there," Sandy said, and went off in a hurry, before Trina could answer, leaving her sitting on the stone wall.

She had done all she could. Sometimes she felt like shaking Trina for being so stupid about herself.

When school was out Sandy tried to keep an eye on Trina, but she managed to slip away. And when the other girls met to wait for Mr. Forster to pick them up, Trina was nowhere to be seen. The four piled into the car and Dad drove them out to the house above Hemlock Road. Melissa, Debra, and Ginger had phoned their mothers and were free for the afternoon. But Sandy continued to feel discouraged. The whole idea of meeting in the cabin was to get Trina to work with them.

When they reached the house, they sat on the porch steps while Dad got out the snowmobile to test it. Mr. Seale had made a trailer sled as well, and Dad hooked that on before he went roaring across the lawn. He circled the house with snow flying on either hand, while the girls watched.

"I wonder why Mr. Seale had a snowmobile?" Sandy mused. "Lots of people think they're awful."

"I know about that," Debra said. "He did hate the way people roar around the countryside in them, breaking fences and making too much noise. Even using them for hunting. But Mr. Seale kept his snowmobile to use for working purposes when he needed to get around on the snow. That's why people had them in the beginning—before they began to use them for fun. It's the only easy way to get up in the woods in winter. He built that trailer so he could carry his saws and tools when the paths had to be cleared of fallen trees, or whatever. Or when he needed to get to his cabin for the work he did there. But he rode only on the trails, and only on his own property."

Dad drew up on the side lawn, pointing toward the trail that wound up the mountain.

As Sandy walked toward the machine, she studied the snow carefully. It stretched unbroken toward the woods, except where the snowmobile had left its ribbed tracks, packing down the snow, and where a file of deep indentations showed where deer had crossed. There were no other marks. No imprints left by Trina's boots to show she might have gone this way.

Mother had put on slacks and a short jacket, and she came out to join the party. When they were ready for the trip through the woods, she sat astraddle of the snowmobile seat right behind Dad, and Melissa and Sandy got into the low trailer. They sat close to the ground, hanging on to the hand grips on either side as they started off. Debra and Ginger stayed behind, waiting for their turn.

Because they were so close to the ground, the speed seemed very great as the snowmobile followed the trail that curved through the woods. After the snowstorm, a marvelous white world stretched away on all sides. Sandy clung to her hand grips, as Mother was doing in front, and tried to watch the wild snowy beauty of the scene as they flashed along the trail with their noise blasting the air. Trees were covered with snow, and there were places where heavy branches arched overhead, so that the snowmobile roared through tunnels of white.

To Sandy's surprise, the deer were not afraid of this noisy blue wagon that sped past. As they rounded a turn,

Sandy saw several deer standing near the hemlock grove, but the animals simply turned their heads and watched with interest as the machine flew past. Apparently, the smell of gasoline frightened them less than the smell of man, and the uproar didn't bother them.

The cabin was quickly reached, and Dad made a turn on the cleared ground around it so he could face the other way for the return trip. Sandy and Melissa climbed out, and for once even Melissa seemed laughing and happy. The ride had been fun.

They stood watching while Dad and Mother sped back through the woods to pick up the other two girls who waited at the house. Melissa started toward the cabin and Sandy followed more slowly, studying the ground. She found what she was looking for almost at once. A track of footprints came out of the woods, not following the path, but having taken a roundabout way through the woods. They marched across the clearing in front of the cabin and went up the snow-piled steps.

Melissa did not notice. She pulled open the door and went into the cabin, with Sandy right on her heels. Across the room Trina knelt at the hearth, setting logs for a new fire, lighting a match, while the little mongrel, Charlie, sprang toward the door to yap at the newcomers. Melissa pushed him away with her foot, as Mrs. Haines had done.

Trina did not look around as Melissa and Sandy came in, and they stood watching her for a moment. Sandy felt anxious and uncertain, wondering how Trina would behave this time. Then Melissa began to stamp snow from her boots on the bare floor, and Sandy went to the fireplace to stand beside Trina. Charlie circled the room, watching them suspiciously.

"Hello, Trina," Sandy said. "I'm glad you came. But we could have brought you up with the snowmobile. Dad's using Mr. Seale's trailer."

Trina said nothing, concentrating on the fire. When the kindling had caught and small flames licked up into the birch logs, she rose and turned around.

"The room will be warm soon," she said.

To Sandy's surprise, she didn't sound angry over their presence, though perhaps she was a little defiant—as though she expected the other two to challenge her in some way. Melissa watched her uneasily, and Sandy wondered how this meeting was ever to work out, with the trouble Trina always seemed to stir up around her.

To break a silence that grew too long, Sandy spoke again to Trina. "The last time I climbed the mountain to come up here, I passed a tree that had long scratches down the trunk, and pieces of bark lying on the ground. What sort of animal would do that? I'd like to write about it in my report."

"I know the one you mean," Trina said. "That's a bear tree. Bears often do that in the woods. Perhaps to get at the ants and insects that may hide under the bark."

"Bears?" Melissa echoed in disbelief. "Bears up here?"

"Why not?" Trina demanded. "They haven't all been killed off or driven away. There are still a few around where there are woods. The foresters see them sometimes. They even come down now and then to have a look at garbage cans near houses. The way raccoons do at night. They're black bears in this part of the country. There used to be lots of them in the old days. They don't bother anyone if you let them alone. If one saw you, he'd just trot off into the woods. That is, unless you threatened him in some way, or threatened a she-bear's cubs. Or if the bear was hurt. Most wild animals aren't dangerous if you leave them alone."

Melissa still did not believe. "Have you ever seen a bear up here?" she asked Trina.

"No, and neither did Mr. Seale. But we could tell by that tree that one had been around."

They could hear the snowmobile returning, roaring up the trail, and they looked out the door as it circled the cabin and came to a stop in front. Debra and Ginger tumbled from the trailer, laughing, and the snowmobile rushed off toward home, with Mother clinging tightly to the hand grips, and Dad standing up to ease the machine around a turn.

Charlie had dashed out the door when it was opened, and he was rushing around excitedly, sniffing at something in the snow. Debra was on the far side of the clearing, clumping through deeper snow as if she wanted to test her boots, and her attention was caught by what Charlie was investigating.

"Hey, look!" she called.

Melissa and Sandy had not yet taken off their coats and they ran across the clearing and looked where Debra was

pointing. An animal had made deep marks in the surface
of the snow. Some of its tracks were quite visible where
snow had blown away and the surface was thin. Sandy
stared in fascination at large imprints of a pad and long,
clawlike toes. Here was something for her track collection.

But Debra was not interested in the tracks alone. She
pointed dramatically at something else that marked the
snow.

"That," she said, "looks like blood."

The stains were bright crimson against the whiteness,
and they looked shiny wet in the sunlight. The girls stared
at one another, and then Sandy ran to the cabin door.

"Trina!" she called. "Trina, come and look!"

Trina did not wait to put on her coat and boots. She
ran across the space the snowmobile had flattened in front
of the cabin and bent over the tracks that marked the
snow beyond them, studying the stains. Then she reached
out a finger and touched the red spot. Charlie went practically crazy barking, and Trina caught hold of his collar as
she held up her finger, reddened at the tip. She looked up
and spoke in a voice that commanded.

"Go back in the cabin, all of you! Here, Charlie! Come
here, boy—we've got to go inside."

12

The Battle of Trina Carpozi

The girls obeyed at once, and Trina came in last, pulling Charlie with her and closing the door behind. Sandy and the others looked at her questioningly.

"Bear tracks," she said shortly. "And that bear has been wounded."

Charlie barked and ran to the door, as though he knew what was out there, and meant to be on guard.

"What have you got that silly dog here for?" Melissa asked. "Is he going to help us on the committee?"

There was no laughter. The others were concentrating on what they had seen outdoors.

"Those hunters yesterday—" Sandy began.

Trina nodded. "Yes. We have to let the game warden know. Otherwise the poor thing may wander around for days and die of his suffering."

"Maybe it's only a little wound," Debra said. "Maybe it will get well by itself."

"We can't be sure of that," said Trina.

"But what shall we do?" There was a note of fright in Ginger's voice.

"Stay here for now," Trina decided. "That stain was wet—it hadn't frozen yet. Which means the bear must have been here only a few minutes ago. If he was wounded yesterday, he may keep opening the wound when he moves around, which could be awfully painful. He could be dangerous now. Sandy, will your father come back to pick us up in the snowmobile?"

Sandy shook her head. "He said it would be all right to walk home when we were through. There's no way to get him to come after us, unless one of us walks back."

"Then we'll just wait for a while," Trina said. "When we leave, we'll all go together. That way, he's less likely to bother us. But first we'll give him time to get away from here."

Melissa was shivering. "I don't want to stay here with a wild bear running around outside. I want to go home."

"Don't be a baby," Trina said. "You have to stay."

Melissa grew red with anger, but the other girls were staring at her, and she walked to a window, turning her back on the room.

Debra and Ginger exchanged helpless looks, while Trina regarded them all impatiently.

"Well?" she said. "You came here for a meeting, didn't you? So go ahead and have it! A bear can't open the door and come in."

Melissa drew back from the window she had pressed against. "He could break a window if he wanted to."

"Perhaps he could, but I don't think he will," Trina told her. "He can't smell us inside the cabin. Wild animals depend more on a sense of smell than on anything else. Perhaps that's why they're not much afraid of machines. There's no man smell."

Trina's suggestion was a good one, and Sandy decided she had better take charge. After all, this was her father's cabin, her father's woods—her father's bear?—so she was the hostess, in a sense. And Trina was right—this would give them something to do. She went to the round wooden table and pulled out a chair.

"Let's get started," she said, trying to sound sure of herself in spite of her horrid awareness of a bear roaming the woods nearby.

This was too much for Melissa. First Trina had taken charge, and now Sandy was directing their actions. She came over and rested her hands on the table, scowling.

"Do you know what I think?" she demanded. "I think Trina's making all this up. She'd like to scare us to get even. I don't think there's any old bear out there at all. And pretty soon I'm going back to the house."

"Oh, no!" Debra cried. "You saw the tracks—and the blood, and—"

"Other animals make tracks. Other animals could leave blood stains if they were hurt. Trina just wants to get back at us. Don't you, Trina?"

"Go out if you want to," Trina said indifferently, and took up her post by a window.

Melissa did not go out. Instead, she threw herself crossly down on a bunk and stretched full length.

Sandy found herself remembering Mr. Wendel's words.

Because of her father Melissa *had* to be important. She couldn't bear it if she wasn't, but she chose all the wrong ways to gain what she wanted. Oh, well, Sandy thought, she didn't have to like everyone, and she didn't like Melissa. But somehow, for the first time, she was a little sorry for her.

Debra and Ginger, moving uncertainly because they were used to following Melissa, sat down at the table and looked expectantly at Sandy. Trina walked about the room watchfully, standing first at one window and then at another. Charlie left the door and followed her anxiously. Perhaps more than anything else, the little dog's behavior convinced Sandy of the bear's presence. Charlie had been terribly excited outside. He had *known*.

Trina spoke over her shoulder. "There's a notebook and pencils in the table drawer."

That was some help. Sandy opened the drawer and drew out a black looseleaf notebook and a rather dull pencil. Mr. Seale had apparently made a few notes at the beginning of the book, but most of the pages were empty. She turned to a blank sheet and began to write down the names of the five girls on the committee, leaving a space under each name. The other two at the table watched her in silence, glancing fearfully toward a window now and then.

Sandy tried to think only about what she was doing. She wanted to put out of her mind that unavoidable moment when they would have to leave this safe, warm room and go out into a forest that was inhabited by a wounded bear. Now and then she too glanced anxiously at a window, not only because of what she might see, but because she knew the afternoon was growing late. The sun had slid down the sky, and the forest around the cabin looked gloomy and dark. They couldn't wait here until the night came. She drew a deep breath and began to talk quickly.

"I've written down all our names," she said. "So now I'm ready to write the topics each of us will take for our reports. Debra, what do you want to study?"

"I thought bears hibernated in the winter," Debra said, paying no attention to Sandy's question.

Again Trina spoke over her shoulder. "They do when the weather gets really cold. But it hasn't been that cold yet. And even in midwinter, when it gets warm, they come out and wander around."

"I'm going to study about animals," Sandy said firmly, and wrote that fact down under her own name. "Pay attention, Debra—what do you choose?"

"What is there to choose?" Ginger said.

Sandy counted on her fingers. "There's the pond—and that means water, as well. There are animals, trees, plants, birds, insects, the air—oh, all sorts of things. We probably won't do the sea, since we're so far inland. Mr. Wendel thought these subjects ought to be something we could study firsthand. It means more that way."

"I've already written about the pond," said Melissa, lying on her back with her eyes closed. "I'm not going to do it all over again."

Reluctantly, Sandy wrote "pond" under Melissa's name and nibbled the eraser on her pencil. "I know!" she said. "Trina can take the subject of water, including the pond, and write a lot of things she probably hasn't even told us."

"I don't want to write anything," Trina said.

Sandy drew a deep, exasperated breath. "You're not stupid, Trina, but you're awfully stubborn. You could probably write as well as anybody else if you'd get busy and try. If you want, you can dictate to me, and I'll set down the words—just the way you talked them yesterday. Then you can copy it back into your own writing."

Trina was intrigued in spite of herself. "Do you think that would work?"

"Of course." Sandy pressed her advantage. "But it would be even better if you'd dictate to yourself and set the words down in the first place. After all—that's what we have to do in writing. We think the words first—and then set them down."

"Trina's a goop," said Melissa, not at all helpful.

Ginger said, "I'll take trees. I know a little about different kinds already. And trees help the ecology a lot."

In relief, Sandy wrote the subject under Ginger's name. Debra said she would choose birds, since her mother was a bird watcher and she could get some help here. In fact, since there was a bird feeder right outside one of the cabin windows, she could begin her study of birds now.

"There's more to it than just naming things," Sandy pointed out. "Mr. Wendel said we'd need to know how each species, or natural element, helps everything else. The important thing is how we all have to live together using our surroundings carefully, and not interfering with each other, or spoiling things."

"Are you going to be a teacher when you grow up?" Melissa called across the room. "You sound preachy enough."

Sandy found her resentment rising. "Why don't you help us instead of acting smart?"

"It wasn't my idea to come up here in the first place," Melissa said. "I didn't want to come here and get trapped in a cabin by make-believe bears. It's going to get dark pretty soon, and if you think I'll stay here all night, you're crazy. There's been time for the bear to go off in the woods by now. *If* there is a bear. Let's get out of here!"

Her voice had risen with the last words, but no one moved. The others looked at Trina. Oddly enough, it was Trina they trusted by this time. She stood by a window which faced the trail winding up from the hollow.

"Don't anybody go outside yet," she said.

Ginger giggled nervously. "But Melissa's right—we can't stay here all night."

"And I'm not going to," Melissa said. Apparently she was over her fear of the bear, or had convinced herself that he didn't exist. Her dread of being caught all night in this cabin in the woods was even greater than her fear of a bear she had not seen. She got up and began to pull on her snow pants and boots, slipped into her coat.

"Maybe we'd all better go," Debra said. "Together. Like Trina says."

Trina was emphatic. "Not yet."

Melissa started toward the door. "You just like to be bossy. I can run too fast for any bear to catch me. Besides, I don't think there is one. I'm going home while there's still daylight."

Trina moved toward her across the room. "Wait—the bear is still around. I didn't want to scare you, but I saw him out there a few minutes ago."

"I don't believe you," Melissa said angrily. "I suppose if I try to go outside, you'll show off by shaking me and punching me again? Well, I won't let you!"

Before anyone could stop her, she flung herself out the door and banged it shut behind her. The other four girls ran to a window to watch her go up the trail. She followed the snowmobile tracks, climbing to the ridge, sliding back once in a slippery place. She pulled herself to her feet quickly and turned around to wave in triumph at the cabin window, where the four girls watched. But her hand froze in midair, and she stood utterly still while a look of horror came over her face.

Sandy pressed against the window, gazing in the direction in which Melissa stared. And as she watched, a huge, shaggy black creature lumbered out of the woods between the cabin and the girl on the slope above. He was moaning and growling as he came, loud enough for those in the cabin to hear, and he dragged one hind leg which left blood stains on the snow.

Trina flung herself toward the door and opened it. "Run, Melissa! Run for home!" Beside her, Charlie began to bark.

But Melissa, white and shaking, did not move. She stood frozen with fear, staring at the bear with terror in her eyes, and had no ability to run.

The bear had seen her. He made a growling sound and began to lumber toward her, moving more quickly now, in spite of his wounded leg.

Trina stayed in the doorway, her gaze never wavering from Melissa and the bear. She kept one hand on Charlie's collar to keep him from dashing out the door.

"Give me some firewood—quick!" she called to the girls behind her.

Sandy ran to the basket of logs, picked up several stout sticks of wood and carried them to Trina. The other girl took one stick in each hand and went out into the snow. Charlie rushed after her.

"Trina, come back!" Debra wailed, but Trina paid no attention. She was stalking the bear, coming up behind him, though still at a distance.

From the open doorway Sandy watched, not feeling the cold, not having time to think or feel anything—only watching in dreadful fascination.

When she was close enough, Trina raised a stick of firewood and threw it at the bear. It struck him in the center of his back, but he kept right on his way, lumbering on toward the foolish, frozen Melissa. The next log Trina threw struck him on his wounded leg, and this time he turned around with a snarl of pain and saw Trina. Here was his tormentor. Here was the enemy he need to kill. Charlie began to bark wildly.

"Run, Melissa!" Trina screamed, and this time Melissa

came to life and flew out of sight over the ridge, following the trail back to the house.

Trina too was running—toward the cabin—but Sandy knew about Trina. She could never move quickly because of her bad foot. She wasn't any good at running, and she was sure to stumble and fall.

Charlie rushed into action, hurling himself toward the shaggy black creature that dwarfed him completely, barking as he attacked. Sandy hesitated only a moment longer. Then, as the little dog darted in, snapping at the bear's feet, and darting away, she ran out the door and across the snow to the awkwardly stumbling girl. She caught Trina by the arm, pulling her along, dragging her by sheer force toward the cabin. She hadn't known she could be so strong. She did not dare look behind to see how close the bear might be, but simply dragged Trina to the door and pushed her through it. Then she stumbled into the room after her and fell to her knees as Debra slammed the door and shot the bolt. It was only seconds later that the bear hurled himself against the closed door, with a force that shook the cabin, clawing at it in an effort to reach his enemy.

"Charlie!" Trina cried. "Where is Charlie?"

Only Debra had seen what happened, and she told Trina in a choked voice.

"The bear struck him with his paw and knocked him away before he came chasing you."

Trina ran to a window, but not even she could go outside, with the bear growling and moaning beyond the door.

Sandy, still on her knees, suddenly began to cry in reaction to her fright. She couldn't help herself. Tears streamed down her face, and her breath came in hiccuping sobs.

Debra put an arm about her. "Don't cry, Sandy. It's all right now. He can't get in. And Melissa's gone for help."

Outside, the bear clawed at the rough bark of the cabin walls, moving away from the door.

"I'm so s-s-scared!" Sandy wailed, and could not stop her chattering teeth.

Ginger went to get her a drink of water from one of the jugs Mr. Seale kept in the cabin, and Sandy sipped it gratefully. While Ginger and Debra fussed over Sandy, Trina stood at the window, trying to see Charlie. After a while

Sandy's tears stopped and she spoke to Trina in a voice that shook a little.

"You saved Melissa's life," she said. "You were awfully brave."

Trina paid no attention. "I think the bear has gone off into the woods," she reported.

A moment later they heard a whining at the door, and Trina ran to fling it open. Charlie came in, shivering and crying, and Trina caught him up in her arms, heedless of the blood that streaked his ribs. When she had examined the wound, she got the first-aid kit that Mr. Seale had stored in the cabin and took care of washing the wound and covering it with a square of bandage.

Sandy had recovered from her fright and she joined the other girls in watching anxiously as Trina tended the little dog. If Trina had saved Melissa, Charlie had probably saved both Trina and Sandy.

They could hear the snowmobile coming long before it topped the ridge, and Sandy thought she had never heard anything more wonderful than its air-splitting roar. She was at the door by the time it slowed its speed and came down the hill to the hollow. This time the trailer was empty and Mother had not come. Dad sat in front with his hands on the steering bar, while Melissa rode behind. She held Dad's shotgun braced with its butt between one foot and the snowmobile, its muzzle under her arm pointing skyward behind, while she hung on to the hand grips on each side of the seat.

The moment the snowmobile stopped, Dad jumped off, grabbed the empty shotgun and began to take shells out of his pocket.

"Get inside!" he told Melissa.

When the gun was loaded, he came to the door to see if everyone was all right.

"Sandy's mother is calling the game warden," he told them. "But I'm going to take a look around in the meantime. I can see bear tracks leading into the woods."

When he'd gone, Melissa bounded into the room, excited and pleased with herself.

"That was the right thing to do!" she cried. "I got help for us all. So now we won't be caught here after dark."

"You also nearly got yourself and Trina mauled by the bear," Sandy pointed out. "If it hadn't been for Trina—"

Melissa fairly snapped at her. "If it hadn't been for

Trina, none of this would have happened. Why did she let me go out the door if she knew there was a bear out there? You might know she'd do something stupid that would get someone hurt!"

There was an intense silence in the room. The other girls stared at Melissa in something like disbelief. Sandy started to protest, but she was so angry the words choked in her throat.

"And that silly dog!" Melissa went on, more derisive than ever. "To go yapping out as though he could do anything about a bear!"

Something strange seemed to happen in the room. Sandy could feel it with all her senses. There was a drawing apart from Melissa, a drawing aside. Debra and Ginger hardly seemed to move, yet they had left their places to stand closer to Trina. Each girl wore an expression that shut Melissa out. No one needed to say anything. Melissa suddenly stood alone, as Trina had once stood alone. No one wanted her for a friend anymore. Debra, who was always gentle when she took time to think, was the first to speak.

"Charlie did help with the bear, Melissa. He's a pretty fine dog." Then she turned to Trina. "Will you help me if I do my report on birds?"

For once Trina understood. For once she leaped to no wrong conclusion, but knew that Debra's words meant an offer of peace—and of real respect. Yet the battle was not entirely over for Trina. She nodded at Debra without answering and returned to her window post to watch for Dad. She still held Charlie in her arms, comforting him.

Melissa stood alone in the middle of the room—and at last she knew what had happened. Perhaps she even felt a little frightened.

In a few moments Dad returned to the cabin. "The bear has gone off into thick woods," he said. "I'll leave him to the game warden. He's bleeding badly, and I expect he'll have to be shot."

"That's what hunters can do," Trina said angrily. "That bear wasn't hurting anything. He was only living his own life."

"Does this mean we can't come up in the woods anymore?" Sandy asked.

Dad shook his head. "I think it will be all right once the game warden tracks this fellow down and has a good look around. I expect he was a visitor. I doubt if there's another bear in these woods. It's unusual to see one in this area. But now suppose I get you girls home. It's beginning to get dark. Who wants to go first?"

Sandy hung back. "Take them," she said, waving her hand at Debra, Ginger, and Melissa. "Trina and I will come last."

After Dad had gone outside, Ginger and Debra stopped at the door, to look back, smiling at Sandy and Trina. Melissa had no smiles for anyone. She went off looking subdued and rather miserable. Poor Melissa, Sandy thought unexpectedly.

The snowmobile roared away, and the cabin in the woods grew very still. The room was shadowy with fading daylight and on the hearth the fire had burned to a few red embers. Without a word, Trina set Charlie down and got water to put out the embers. Sandy discovered that she had stopped being hot with anger and was growing cold. She began to put on her outdoor things.

Trina watched her for a moment. Then she rose from the hearth and went to the drawer under the bunk. Carefully she took out her treasure box and brought it to the table. When the cover was off she reached inside and took something out—something she brought to Sandy. It was the small lily-of-the-valley carving Trina's mother had made long ago and given to her daughter.

"It's for you," Trina said gruffly.

Sandy understood. The gift meant a great many things that Trina could not say. It meant a turnabout in her road, for one thing. By accepting it, Sandy would seal a bond of friendship between them. And she knew now how much Trina's friendship was worth having. Perhaps later on she would find a way to give the carving back—because it meant so much to Trina. But for a little while she would keep it.

"Thank you," she said softly.

When Trina smiled, her green eyes came to life, and here was nothing lumpish about her.

"Tomorrow I'm going to see your grandparents," Sandy said. "I'm going to tell them what you did to save Melissa, and about how much you're helping us with the ecology project."

Trina's smile vanished and she scowled in the old way. "Oh, no, you won't!" she cried.

Sandy only laughed at her. "Saying, 'Oh, no, I won't,' and, 'Oh, no, you won't'—that's a very stupid way to get anywhere. And you're not a stupid girl."

Trina looked at her, but the scowl faded and she seemed somehow relieved. As though she might have wanted all along to have someone stop her from going down that foolish road.

With a moment of insight, Sandy recognized several things. Everything wouldn't necessarily be fine from now on. Trina would always be difficult—and—*different*. Perhaps it was a good thing for some people to be different.

"There comes the snowmobile," Trina said and put on her own coat and boots.

They went out of the darkening cabin and watched the bright headlights of the machine come over the rise. When it drew to a stop after circling the cabin, they both climbed into the trailer and hung on tight, Trina holding Charlie between her feet.

The night roared with sound and the headlights cut a glowing path through snowy woods. On either side the forest vanished into blackness as they swept past, swaying around the curves, sending the snow flying.

For some reason, perhaps because of the snowy trees, Sandy thought about Christmas. She knew what she was going to give Trina for a present. Somewhere she would find a bottle of lily-of-the-valley perfume for Trina Carpozi.

She felt quite dreamy with contentment when the snowmobile made its last dash across the lawn toward the house. There were lights in the windows, and Mother stood in the doorway waiting to welcome them home. The other girls seemed to have gone.

"Come along in," Sandy said to Trina. "We have to tell my mother about what's happened."

But she stood for a moment longer outside before she went toward the door, looking up at the star-filled night, and at the gleam of starshine on the pond. She knew now what that word "ecology" meant. It meant a treasuring of the earth and a sharing of it with all living things. It was as simple as that—and as hard.

Trina was waiting for her. They went inside together.

About the Author

PHYLLIS A. WHITNEY was born of American parents in Yokohama, Japan, where her father was in business. Later the family lived in the Philippines and China. After her father's death, she and her mother returned to the States, which she saw for the first time at age fifteen. In this country she has lived in Berkeley, San Antonio, and Chicago, and presently resides on Long Island, New York.

Phyllis Whitney has been writing since the age of fifteen, first short stories and then her first book in 1941. To date she has published over fifty novels, many of which are for young people. Her books have been translated into seventeen languages, with millions of copies in paperback and hardcover in more than two hundred editions. In recent years she has published some eighteen adult suspense novels. Her own daugher loved to read her books when she was growing up, and now enjoys the adult novels. Phyllis Whitney's three grandchildren are presently following in their mother's footsteps.

The author has spent much time in travel, with many of her books set in areas she has visited or lived in. She works six days a week at her writing, usually mornings from 8 to 11; after time out in midday, she returns to writing until 4:30 or 5.

She has won a number of awards for her books for young people, twice receiving the "Edgar" Award of the Mystery Writers of America. She spent a year with the Chicago Public Library and has been Children's Book Editor for both *The Chicago Sun* and *The Philadelphia Inquirer*. She was instructor in Juvenile Fiction Writing at Northwestern University and taught for eleven years at New York University. Presently all her time is given to writing, usually two books a year, one for young people and one for adults.